Endangered

Books by Kate Jaimet

Endangered
Edge of Flight
Break Point
Slam Dunk
Dunces Anonymous
Dunces Rock

Endangered

Kate Jaimet

The Poisoned Pencil

An imprint of Poisoned Pen Press

First Edition 2015

10 9 8 7 6 5 4 3 2 1

Library of Congress Catalog Card Number: 2014958054

ISBN: 9781929345168 Trade Paperback
9781929345175 E-book

The Poisoned Pencil
An imprint of Poisoned Pen Press
6962 E. First Ave., Ste. 103
Scottsdale, AZ 85251
www.thepoisonedpencil.com
info@thepoisonedpencil.com

Printed in the United States of America

To the *New Brunswick Telegraph-Journal*
Moncton bureau crew, 1997–'98

Acknowledgments

The author would like to gratefully acknowledge the support of the Ontario Arts Council, which provided a grant to aid in the writing of this book.

ONTARIO ARTS COUNCIL
CONSEIL DES ARTS DE L'ONTARIO

an Ontario government agency
un organisme du gouvernement de l'Ontario

Prologue

I only have one photo of my mother.

It's in a baby album Gram made for me, stuck on a page with my yellowed hospital bracelet and a plastic pocket stuffed with wispy baby hair.

In the picture, my mother is lying in bed wearing a rumpled t-shirt, with the bedspread pulled up just to her waist—like she hit the mattress and fell asleep before she had time to tuck herself in properly. Beneath the picture is written: *Shauna & Hayley, July, 1998.*

Her eyes are closed and her hair is splayed all around her head—not tousled, like in the perfume ads, but just messy, like she went to sleep without blow-drying it, and it's going to take an industrial strength comb to get the tangles out once she wakes up. One of her arms is flung out to the side, the other is curled around her head. There, in the crook below her arm, is where I'm lying: a tiny baby with my eyes closed like hers, and my arm, like hers, curled around my head.

Like two peas in a pod, Gram might have said.

Except Gram would never say that about me and my mom.

Her hair is jet-black, like mine is now, though in the picture I have duckling-down baby hair. Her cheekbones are high and slanted like mine are too. They look exotic, here in the land of Celtic descendants. Slavic, maybe. Or maybe Native. Who knows? Like so much else about her, I haven't gotten to the truth of that.

When I was little, I used to daydream that my mother was a Russian princess, kidnapped by an evil prince to his castle in faraway Siberia. I would imagine the prince dying in a war and my mother returning to Canada to fetch me. She would tell me how she'd climbed mountains and crossed rivers and fought dragons because her love for me was so strong she could not bear for us to be parted.

I gave up on those fantasies when I hit my teens and started hanging out in my father's newsroom—hearing bits and pieces from the reporters about what happened between her and my dad. By the winter I hit sixteen, I was working for the paper on weekends. Then last summer, I started helping out the cop reporter on the crime beat, and I'd never really looked back. Since then I'd seen enough of the gritty underside of Halifax to realize that stories of pregnant teenage party-girls don't usually have fairy-tale endings.

But sometimes I still wonder where those cheekbones came from—hers and mine. There must have been other pictures, once upon a time. Pictures of her holding me. Pictures of her with my dad, together. Maybe even pictures of her with her parents.

My theory is that Dad threw them all away, but Gram salvaged one for the baby book. Just one. This one.

Maybe she saved it because it makes my mother looks so innocent: Her eyes closed, her newborn child nestled beside her.

One

The call came through at six thirty a.m. Some cops had found a blood-splattered shack, off a country road in the scrubby woodlands east of Halifax.

"Looks like we're going to need Major Crime out here," I heard an officer tell dispatch through the crackly static of the newsroom scanner.

"Copy that. Are you in danger?"

"Negative. The place looks empty. Couple of ATVers stumbled across it in the middle of the night."

"Copy that...*static*...What is your 10-20?"

I wrote down the details of the location in my notepad as the cop gave directions to the dispatcher. Then I grabbed a Diet Coke from the fridge beside the copydesk. Normally, I laid off the caffeine a few hours before the end of my overnight shift. But it looked like bedtime might be delayed that morning. Especially if the cops found a body.

To be honest, I was surprised there hadn't been more action on the police scanner that night. Most of the high schools in Halifax—including mine—had held their proms last evening, and I'd expected at least one drunk-driving accident to punctuate my night shift. But then, what did I know about high-school graduation parties? I wasn't entitled to graduate, thanks to a bombed biology exam that nixed my chances at a diploma from Sir Robert Borden High School—aka Boredom High. So while the rest of my classmates were glitzing it up in the Lord Nelson Hotel ballroom, I'd been sitting in the newsroom all night, updating the paper's website with overseas wire-copy, monitoring the police scanner, and checking Facebook every ten minutes to see which of my friends were making out, breaking up, or getting hammered.

Yeah, I would've liked to have been at the prom. But I couldn't have cared less about a high school graduation certificate. The only piece of paper I wanted to hang on my wall was a National Newspaper Award.

I stuffed my phone, notepad, and digital recorder into my purse, grabbed my camera, picked up the phone on my desk and dialed the first digit of Tenzen's number. I thought twice and hung up the phone again.

Not that Tenzen would mind being dragged out of bed at six thirty a.m. to check out a blood-covered shack in the woods. The grizzled old cop reporter lived for that kind of stuff. In fact, he'd expect me to call him. Just like I'd expect him to call me if a murder story broke on his shift—send me knocking on doors in hopes of finding an eyewitness, or assign me to cover the police press conference while he pumped his off-the-record sources for the inside scoop. For the past year, I'd been Tenzen's unofficial apprentice. I had nothing to complain about. I'd learned a lot of stuff and skipped a lot of classes—which explained why I'd bombed that biology exam. But whenever a big crime story appeared in the paper, the byline always read: By Rod Tenzen. Then, way at the bottom, in italic letters: *with files from Hayley Makk.*

Not this time. This was my shift. My story. My byline. I could handle it on my own.

I sank into the driver's seat of my '98 Pontiac Firefly and cranked up some tunage to keep me awake on the drive to the crime scene. I'd trashed my savings account to buy the car as a non-graduation gift to myself after I got the results of my biology final. If I was going to keep living at home while other kids went off to university, at least I deserved my own set of wheels. It was a three-cylinder convertible with an orange paint-job that camouflaged the rust around the wheel wells, with a tape deck instead of a CD player. After I'd gotten it home, I'd dragged out a cardboard box filled with my dad's cassette tapes to see if I could find anything worth listening to. I'd rescued a couple of albums by The Clash but the rest was lame old people's music—Madonna, Boyz II Men, Celine Dion. Seriously. Celine Dion.

It was one of those gray Halifax mornings where the peaks of the Victorian rooftops poke through the fog like a scene from a cheesy teenage vampire movie. I turned into the empty downtown streets to the opening drum roll of "I Fought the Law" and reached the highway on-ramp by the song's final crescendo.

There wasn't much traffic except for the occasional logging truck or heavy rig, but I kept an eye out all the same. There were bound to be a few bleary-eyed grads on the road, trying to make it home from the after-hours parties before their parents woke up and found them AWOL.

The rising sun made a smudgy gray thumbprint in the overcast sky. Shreds of fog clung to the tree branches and the early summer cornstalks in the fields. About thirty minutes out of Halifax, I turned on to Concession Road 14 as per the cop's directions, passed some rocky sheep-pastures and drove through the wooded hinterland until I spotted a cruiser parked on the dirt shoulder. The Clash was rocking the Casbah as I pulled up behind it. I took a last gulp of Diet Coke and got out of the Firefly, scuffing my combat boots in the pebbles of the road's shoulder.

Two cops stood at the entrance to a narrow dirt path, which was tied off with yellow police tape. The older one was big and beefy, with a cleft chin and gelled gray hair. He looked ticked off that someone had the nerve to stick a crime-scene out here in the godforsaken woods—and at the end of his night shift at that.

The second cop looked friendlier. I guessed he wasn't much older than some of the guys in my class—though I knew you had to be nineteen to join the Mounties—which made him two years older than me. He had the body of an athlete, an oval face, and a brown forelock that fell in a fringe over his left eyebrow. I figured I'd try my luck with him, rather than attempting to strike up a conversation with Officer Beefy over there.

"Morning, Officer. Hayley Makk, *Halifax Independent*." I flashed my notepad at him. "Can I ask you what's going on here?"

The young cop didn't say anything, but turned to look at his partner.

Sergeant Beefy shrugged one shoulder.

"Talk to Media Relations," he growled.

Thanks for nothing.

I made a point of looking at my watch. "Yeah, it's seven-thirty. The Media Relations desk doesn't open till eight."

The beefy cop shrugged both shoulders this time. Maybe he was making twice the effort to respond. Or maybe he was doubly indifferent. Whatever the case, it wasn't helping me get a story.

"I heard on the scanner something about a shack, covered in blood," I said.

"Whatever you heard, you heard."

Thanks for nothing. Again.

"Can you tell me who owns this property, Officer?"

"Land registry office opens at nine," Sergeant Beefy grunted. He gave me a look like I was too young to play reporter, and I should be home listening to lame pop music and texting my boyfriend.

Maybe I should've called Tenzen, after all.

"Yeah, so I could go look it up, right?" I said. "So why don't you just tell me? I won't quote you. Promise."

Sergeant Beefy stared straight ahead, like he'd developed an overwhelming interest in the scrawny birch trees across the road. I had an urge to duck under the police tape and make a break for the cabin to get a front page photo, but I had a feeling he'd tackle me like a linebacker the instant I set foot on the path.

The young cop shot me a glance of what seemed like sympathy. He probably had to deal with a lot of attitude from Sergeant Beefy on a regular basis. I gave him a little smile, like: *Hey, I get it, my editor's just as hard-assed as your partner, and he's gonna chew me out if I go back to the newsroom without a story, so do you think you could give me a little break here?*

The young cop glanced at his partner, whose eyes were still glued on the scenery across the road. He pulled a notepad out of his breast pocket and flipped a couple of pages.

"Chiasson," he said. "Her-me-ne-gilde."

His tongue stumbled over the old-fashioned name.

"How do you spell that?" I asked.

"I don't." He cracked a grin.

Cute. Very cute.

"Anything else you can tell me?" I wasn't expecting much, but the young cop nodded his head to the side, indicating a couple of teenage guys sitting on a log in the woods, about fifty feet away.

"Those guys. They found the place last night. You'll want to hurry, though. One of their moms is on her way to pick them up."

"Thanks, Constable," I looked at his name tag, "Turpin." I handed him my business card.

"Pleasure," he nodded, tucking the card away in his breast pocket. "Don't quote me."

I tromped through the woods in the direction he'd indicated. Birds chirped in the trees, trying to convince me that this was all a scene from a Disney movie, but the two guys sitting on the log didn't look like charming princes. As I got closer, I recognized them from my class in school: Phil Brewer and Chuck West.

Phil's lanky blond hair fell in a dirty tangle around his chalk-pale face. He wore a once-white dress shirt and black dress pants, caked to the knees in mud. Chuck had an Irving Oil baseball cap shoved backwards on top of his mess of brown hair and wore the same style of black pants and white shirt as his friend. But he was glammed up with a purple cummerbund and a purple bow tie that clung crookedly to his collar, barely hanging on through what had obviously been a rough night.

"Hey, guys."

"Hey, Hayley," said Phil.

Chuck didn't say anything. He looked like he was going to barf if he opened his mouth.

"Rough night?"

Phil nodded: "Yeah."

"Cops said you found a shack in the woods, covered in blood."

"Yeah," said Phil.

"Totally covered," added Chuck, looking green.

"I'm writing about it. For the paper."

"Oh. Cool," said Phil.

"So, can you tell me what happened?"

Phil shrugged.

"I dunno. We just found it."

"Okay. How'd you find it?"

"We were out ATVing."

"This was after the grad party?"

"Kind of. Chuck's girlfriend dumped him."

"At the dance," Chuck put in.

I knew the girl he'd been dating, Clarissa, a semi-hysterical princess-type. It would've been totally typical of her to dump a guy at the prom. Probably didn't like his purple cummerbund.

"Bummer," I said.

"'Salright," Chuck mumbled.

"So, I took him out ATVing, eh?" Phil continued.

"We were kinda drinking," Chuck added.

"'Cause, what else are you gonna do?" said Phil.

"Right," I said.

"So then the machine gets stuck in the mud, eh?"

"Swamp," Chuck corrected him.

"Whatever. We were kinda lost…"

"And drunk," Chuck put in.

"And then we found this shack. So it was like, let's just crash here. And when we woke up…"

"Holy shit," said Chuck.

"Holy shit," said Phil.

"Holy shit, what?"

"Blood," said Chuck. "Blood everywhere."

"It was all over the walls and all over the floor and everything. I mean, I been in hunting cabins before where there might be some dried blood on the counter or the table, eh? But this was everywhere."

"Gory," said Chuck.

I scribbled the quotes in my notepad.

"So, what'd you do after that?"

"Puked," said Chuck.

"Right," I said. "And afterwards?"

"Hiked out to the highway," said Phil. "There was this trail and besides, we could hear the traffic. So we flagged down a trucker, eh? And he called the cops."

"What'd the cops say?"

"They asked us a ton of questions. Then they said they were gonna call some more investigators."

"Okay. Thanks, guys."

I got them to pose for a couple of pics, while a police van pulled up and some men who must have been crime-scene investigators got out. Just as I was finishing up taking pics, a blue SUV pulled on to the shoulder of the road near the cop cars. A lady in a tracksuit got out and made a beeline for the cops. She looked jumped-up on stress, with a bad case of bed-head.

"That's my mom," said Chuck.

"Okay. Call me if you hear anything else." I gave him one of my business cards, then headed back to the Firefly. I figured it was best to leave the scene before parental authority showed up and advised the kids not to speak to the media.

Besides, I had my quotes. I had pics. I had enough for a story. Maybe a front page story.

Heading back toward Halifax on Concession Road 14, I passed a white CBC-TV van making for the crime scene. But the SUV carrying Chuck and his buddy was already on the road behind me, and I doubted the cops would give the CBC any more information than they'd given me. I recognized the reporter driving the van and waved as we crossed paths.

Ha. I thought. *Scooped ya.*

Two

As soon as I got back to the newsroom, I posted a quick news-hit on the website along with a photo of Phil and Chuck. I spent the next hour calling every H. Chiasson in the phone book, hoping to hit on the owner of the property. I talked to three Henri's, a Herman, a Hervé, and a Henriette, but no Hermenegilde; and no one who knew anything about a bloody shack on Concession Road 14.

I was just getting off the phone with Henriette—who'd given me the rundown of all her relatives from Bathurst to Cheticamp and not a Hermenegilde among them—when a mug of coffee landed on my desk, followed by a leg dressed in cream-colored linen. My dad—a.k.a. the editor-in-chief of the *Halifax Independent*.

"Good work on that story, Hayley. We beat CBC on the pic of the witnesses." He took a slug of coffee. "Anything else happen last night?"

"Nah, that's it," I said. "We're out of Diet Coke."

"What do I look like, a vending machine?" said Dad. "Okay, write a roll-over note to Tenzen. He'll follow the story on dayside. Then—"

My cell phone rang, interrupting Dad's instructions. He glanced at it, then at me.

"Could be a source," I said, thinking of cute Constable Turpin, and the way he'd tucked my business card into his breast pocket. *Pleasure...* Dad motioned for me to take the call.

"Hayley Makk, *Halifax Independent*."

It wasn't Constable Turpin, but a blast from my past at Boredom High.

"Hayley? This is Ms. Cameron. Nora Cameron? Your biology teacher?"

She raised her voice at the end of the sentences, like maybe I'd forgotten her in the four weeks since classes ended. But how could I forget the person who'd cancelled out my four years of high school with a brutally hard final exam?

"Hi, Ms. Cameron," I said. Dad raised an eyebrow, recognizing the teacher's name. "You caught me in the newsroom. Don't tell me someone blew up the chemistry lab."

Her sigh weighed down the telephone.

"You should try reading more *National Geographic* and less *National Enquirer*, Hayley. It would broaden your mind."

"Hey, if it bleeds it leads, Ms. Cameron."

"Perhaps I should talk directly to your father."

"That's okay, you can talk to me. What's up?"

Dad, obviously figuring it could take a while, motioned that I should come and see him in his office after the call was over. I dragged my mind away from the bloody shed on Concession Road 14, and tried to focus on my ex-biology teacher.

She gave me the lowdown about some strange sea turtle she'd seen a couple of days ago when she was out kayaking in the Eastern Islands. She was so worked up about it, she'd hired an old fishing boat and its captain, and was planning to spend a couple of weeks doing research on the thing.

"This could be an opportunity for you to experience some groundbreaking herpetofaunal research," she enthused.

"Herpeto-what?" It sounded like a sexually transmitted disease.

"Herpetofaunal, Hayley," she sighed. "Reptiles and amphibians are classified as herpetofauna. From the Greek word *herpetos*, meaning 'crawling.'"

"Right." I hated to tell her, but groundbreaking herpetofaunal research wasn't exactly front page news at the *Halifax Independent*. Dad built the paper every day on a bedrock of crime and hockey coverage, with some politics and human interest planted on top to gussy it up and broaden the readership appeal.

"We don't really have a science and nature beat, Ms. Cameron," I said.

"Oh, I'm not talking about a newspaper story," she answered. "Listen, Hayley, I've discussed this with the principal, and if you were to participate in the research, your report on the project could be counted in lieu of a final exam. I could use the help, and it would be a chance for you to finish your grade twelve biology credit. You're a bright girl, Hayley. I think you deserve a chance to get your high school diploma."

My high school diploma. Like that was supposed to be an enticement.

"I'm doing fine without it."

"I can see you are, Hayley, but...doesn't your father own the paper?"

"Yeah." And he'd given me my job, if that was what she was driving at. Otherwise I'd be out there flipping burgers like any other high school flunky. Not that I was going to admit that to Ms. Cameron.

"He needs me in the newsroom," I added, which happened to be true. Anyone who spent a day at the *Halifax Independent* could see that Dad ran the paper on a shoestring, competing against the *Halifax Chronicle-Herald* with a combination of aggressive reporting, screaming headlines, and a gazillion hours of unpaid overtime. Besides myself, the paper had four news reporters, including Tenzen, a grizzled veteran who'd been around since the days of electric typewriters and wore coke-bottle glasses three times the diameter of his eyeballs. And there was a summer intern, a sports reporter, and a senior political writer at the provincial legislature—in other words, barely enough bodies to cover Halifax's run-of-the-mill crime and controversy without sending reporters out to chase after herpetofauna.

"Why don't you transfer me to your dad, Hayley?" Ms. Cameron said. "I think I should talk to him about this."

"No, I'll talk to him, Ms. Cameron." The last thing I needed was a teacher trying to guilt my dad into sending me back to school. On my one-to-ten list of Ways to Spend My Summer, chasing a potential murder story rated a ten; sailing the seas after Timmy the Turtle fell off the scale into the black abyss on the far side of zero.

"Really, Hayley, I think it's better that I talk to him directly," Ms. Cameron persisted. "I can explain the scope of the research, and answer any questions that he might have."

"Unfortunately, he's busy right now," I gave her the old line. "But I'll talk to him as soon as he's free."

We argued back and forth, and by the time I hung up, I'd promised Ms. Cameron that I'd try to convince Dad to send me back into the clutches of the public education system. It was safe to promise, because Dad was never going to go for it. He'd have to replace me on the night shift, which was a job no-one in the newsroom wanted. Plus, we had a potential murder story on our hands. Plus, he'd dropped out of journalism school himself at the age of twenty to start up the *Independent* with a government grant and Gram's life savings. It was safe to say he was the last dad in the world who would insist on seeing his daughter in a black gown and mortarboard.

I went to see Dad as soon as I'd finished writing the roll-over note to Tenzen, passing on all the info and contacts he'd need to chase the story. By now, the newsroom was starting to buzz: the reporters had arrived for work and the city editor was handing out assignments. There was a City Hall meeting about a downtown development that had the heritage people up in arms, and a story about a lady who claimed her shi-tzu had been eaten by a coyote, out in one of the new suburbs where the wildlife still thought they owned the place. The garbled static of the police scanner completed the background noise.

Dad was sitting with his feet up on his desk, talking on the phone with the receiver jammed between his shoulder and his ear while he answered email on his Blackberry. I waded through the usual jumble of newspapers that littered the floor and rose in messy piles against the walls. So much for the digital era in publishing. Someday he'd be forced to relocate while he called in a guy with a pitchfork and a recycling truck.

I cleared a copy of the *Toronto Sun* off a chair and sat down.

"Tell him we don't want the PR flak! We want to talk to the Minister!" Dad was griping into the phone. "Yeah? Well tell him he's got till end of day to give us his comments. Then we're going to press with this story! Okay. Later."

Dad hung up, swung his feet down, and swiveled to face me. He laid his palms flat on his desk and leaned forward.

"What did your biology teacher want?" he said.

I gave him the gist of my conversation with Ms. Cameron.

"Right," said Dad. "How much time d'you need for this thing? A couple of weeks? A month?"

"Are you kidding me, Dad? You don't really want me to go on this gig, do you?"

"Why not? Might be good. Herpeto-whatever research. Raise the tone of the paper a bit, eh? Make us more highbrow."

"Dad, what are you talking about?"

Dad's idea of highbrow was Cheez Whiz on rye instead of on Wonder bread.

Dad smacked his hand against his forehead.

"What I'm talking about, Hayley, is that any idiot can fail a biology exam. It takes a real moron to skip the makeup test."

"A moron. Thanks, Dad."

"Look, Hayley, you go out there, you write a report about this turtle-thing, and you get your diploma. It's a no-brainer."

"What about my story? It could be a murder case, Dad."

"Tenzen can chase it."

"Tenzen? That's not fair, Dad. I broke that story."

"No, you happened to be sitting at the police scanner when the story broke," Dad said. "Besides, Tenzen's already got his high school diploma."

"So what, Dad? You dropped out of school."

"College, not high school. And besides, I needed to work. I didn't have a choice."

Dad pinned me with his hockey-enforcer stare and I knew he was daring me to drop the gloves: *You want this fight, kid? Come on, let's have this fight.* The fight over why he'd dropped out of school seventeen years ago. The fight over whose fault it was.

Seventeen years ago.

My mom's fault, for getting pregnant.

My fault, for being born.

We'd had this fight before, and I knew how it would go. I'd end up screaming that it wasn't my fault he got her pregnant and she took off when I was a baby, and the words would hurt me as much as they hurt him: She took off when I was a baby. And he'd yell that I didn't appreciate what I had, didn't appreciate how much he and Gram had done for me. It wasn't a fight anyone could ever win, and it wasn't a fight I wanted to have right there in the newsroom, in front of everyone.

"I've already got a job, Dad," I said instead. "I don't need a degree."

"You think this job is forever? Come on, Hayley, you know what's happening in this business. People think they can get any information they want on the Web and guess what? It's free! Everyone and his brother's a bloody blogger. Who needs to buy a newspaper? Advertising's down, cost of newsprint is up. I've got laid-off reporters from the *Daily News* calling me up begging for jobs. I don't even know if we're gonna weather this recession. Christ, CanWest went bankrupt. The *New York Times* is cutting staff. What happens if the *Independent* goes under? Are you going to go out there with a handful of tabloid clippings and compete against kids with university degrees and summer internships at the *Globe and Mail*? Get real, Hayley. You don't want to be a high school dropout your whole life."

A high school dropout your whole life. *Like your mom*, he could have said. But he didn't. I wasn't the only one backing off the big fight.

"I could work for the *Globe and Mail*," I said.

"Yeah? Well, you don't. You work for me. So guess what? I'm sending you on assignment. I want a thousand words on this creature, whatever it is: "Mystery Turtle Terrorizes Eastern Shore."

"Terrorizes?" I swear, my dad was the only guy in the world who deliberately picked the longest checkout line in the supermarket so he could scan the tabloid headlines for inspiration.

"People better be terrorized when they read your story," Dad said. The phone rang and he answered it. "Yeah, Jen, did you get the Minister?"

I got up to go.

"And I want pictures, Hayley!" Dad shouted after me. "Front page pictures!"

Front page pictures of a sea turtle. Fantastic.

Looked like I'd be spending a thrilling summer aboard a smelly fishing boat with my ex-biology teacher. Probably with no cell phone or Internet coverage, either. Tenzen would get my big crime story, and the only thing I'd get was an infection in my eyebrow stud from not showering for a month.

I probably wouldn't be seeing Constable Alex Turpin again, either.

Not that it mattered.

But it never hurts to cultivate a contact on the Force.

Three

I pulled into the foggy parking lot of the Halifax harbor at six-twenty the next morning, when the tide was going out and I should've been sleeping in. The car heater wheezed a thin stream of warm air. I let it run for a few minutes after putting the car in park, while I finished my Diet Coke.

Dad had given me the night off so I'd be well-rested for my amazing herpetofaunal adventure, but my body was still set to vampire time and I hadn't been able to sleep. After a couple hours of tossing and turning, I'd finally gotten out of bed around one a.m., put on my earphones, cranked up the Billy Talent on my iPod, and wailed away on my drumpads for a couple of hours.

I was ready for bed now, but no such luck. I crumpled my Diet Coke can, grabbed my duffle bag, laptop and camera gear from the passenger seat, locked up my car against joy-riders, and headed toward the wharf. The fog wrapped itself around me like a damp dishrag. It was late June, but still not warm enough for the t-shirt and cargo pants I was wearing. A Fair Isle sweater that Gram had knitted was packed in my duffle bag, along with an oil slicker and a pair of rubber boots, but I was saving the outport-fisherman look for later in the expedition, when I'd have no remote chance of bumping into anyone I knew. The air smelled of saltwater, diesel oil, and slimy dead sea-things. Gulls screeched and swooped through the fog.

Ms. Cameron was standing on the wharf next to a pile of scuba gear and duffle bags that were presumably meant to be loaded onto the battered fishing boat that bobbed alongside. She had a multi-pocketed jacket thrown over her usual sweater-and-khakis combo, and her brown hair was pulled back in a ponytail beneath a broad-brimmed rain hat. She had deeply tanned skin and a thin face sprinkled with freckles.

"Hayley!" She stopped loading and smiled at me. "It's great to see you again."

She turned and gestured toward a man in a plaid shirt, who was loading gear onto the boat. The man's body was stocky, his arms knotted with muscles, and his face looked like it had been chipped from rugged crags of Cape Breton.

"This is our captain," she said.

The captain's huge, calloused fingers came crushing down on mine, like he was breaking open a lobster carapace with his bare hand. "Cap'n Gil," he grunted and turned back to his work.

"And I think you know Ernest," continued Ms. Cameron. She gestured at a scrawny kid in baggy hemp pants and a wool poncho, standing off to the side.

I vaguely recognized Ernest from school, though as far as I could remember I'd never talked to him. Ernest had "anti-globalization protestor" written all over him: dark blond hair in dirty dreadlocks, fingernails that could've used a pair of pruning shears, and an outfit that looked like he'd bought it directly from the craftspeople in some small Andean village.

"Hey," I said.

Ernest stared at me, eyes as waxy as an organic turnip.

I was tempted to turn around, get back in my car, and tell Dad I'd missed the tide and the expedition had gone ahead without me. But he'd have a fit if I tried to pull that stunt, take me off the crime beat and send me out to cover the Federation of Nova Scotia Retirees' Golden Needle Knitting Awards. Serve me right for blowing the chance to get my high school diploma, Dad would figure. *Too stupid to know what was good for her. Just like her mother.* He might not say it, but he'd think it. So I hoisted my duffle bag and climbed on board, hoping the turtle would make a quick and spectacular appearance so I could write my story and get the hell out of there.

The boat was a thirty-five-foot fishing vessel, with a pilot-house above deck and a galley below. There was a big hatch in the stern for storing the day's catch, with a winch behind it for raising heavy nets from the sea. Ms. Cameron set Ernest to loading the hatch with wetsuits and scuba gear, while Captain Gil instructed me to store my duffle bag in the galley. I climbed down the narrow ladder, into a dim, low-ceilinged room.

The galley smelled of fish and diesel oil. It looked like a cross between an eat-in kitchen and a floating toolshed—all sorts of vital pieces of safety equipment were fastened to the walls, so that you could barely move without bumping into a hatchet or elbowing a life preserver. A grimy metal stove squatted in one corner. To one side of it stood a stainless-steel sink; to the other a Formica table, bolted to the floor and surrounded on three sides by narrow benches, which were also bolted to the floor. The whole place could have used a fresh coat of paint, not to mention a decorative upgrade from the brown foam-and-vinyl upholstery.

Captain Gil showed me how the seats of the benches hinged open like lids, revealing a storage space underneath for me to stow my personal gear. Blankets and pillows were already stowed there, since the benches would double as beds for Ernest and me, the Captain said. Sounded like a blast—summer sailing camp with crunchy-granola boy.

A small door at the front of the galley led to a tiny, triangular cabin wedged into the bow. That was where Ms. Cameron would sleep. It was already crammed with her personal stuff and a bunch of scientific equipment.

When I got back on deck, a massive burgundy car was pulling up in the foggy parking lot at the base of the wharf. I watched as an old man got out and began walking toward us, the dock creaking under his slow, heavy gait. Ms. Cameron, who had been arranging the scuba gear in the hold, jumped off the boat and hurried toward him.

"Doctor Wallis!"

"Ah, Nora!"

He was gray-haired, big-boned, and gaunt like a starving Clydesdale, with sunken eye sockets and a trench coat that hung loosely from the high, broad ledge of his shoulders. In his right hand, he gripped a hard-shelled plastic case, twice as thick as a briefcase. In his left he held a black cane with a white handle. His voice was deep and wheezy, like a damaged pipe organ.

"Here, let me take that from you," Ms. Cameron began, reaching for the plastic case. Before she could take it, the man doubled over with a heavy, hacking cough, dropped the case and fumbled for a pocket handkerchief.

Ms. Cameron hovered around as though she wanted to help in some way—give him a cough drop or take his blood pressure or something—but in the end, she just picked up the case from the wharf and waited until the coughing fit ended. He straightened up and wiped his mouth.

"My lungs, Nora, don't you see?" He tucked his handkerchief back in to his trench coat pocket. "I'm afraid my days of field research are over."

"It's all right, Doctor Wallis. I'll keep you fully informed of everything we find." Ms. Cameron touched his shoulder.

"Now you mustn't forget to activate the GPS transmitter before you attach it," the old man said. "We mustn't lose contact with the creature. That's absolutely critical. If this turtle is as unusual as you've described..."

"It's what I saw..."

"Then it could be of huge importance. Now, the full instructions are inside the case. Let me just show you..."

Creakily, he lowered himself to one knee and motioned for Ms. Cameron to set the case on the dock. I leaned over to get a better view at whatever high-tech tracking gear the old man had brought. But before Ms. Cameron could unlatch the case, my cell phone rang. Maybe a last-minute reprieve from Dad.

"Hayley Makk."

"Kid!" came a gravelly voice. "You still on terra firma?"

"Tenzen."

I stepped to the other side of the boat so Ms. Cameron wouldn't overhear my conversation. "We're still in harbor. Can you get me out of here?"

"Sorry, kid. Father knows best."

"Whatever."

"Listen, kid. That crime scene yesterday. Anyone mention a guy, name of Tyler Dervish?"

Tyler Dervish. I knew the name, but not from the crime scene. He was a skinny kid with a big Adam's apple, the skin on his face a mess of pimples and scabs. The kind of kid who spent the first few years of high school trying to worm his way into the popular crowd while they all ignored him. Then, when he finally had something they wanted—which, in Tyler's case, was drugs—he acted like a big shot. But everyone knew that he wasn't really a big shot; underneath, he was just the skinny kid with acne, desperate to make friends.

"Why?" I said. "What's Tyler Dervish got to do with anything?"

"Cops found his prints in the blood in that shack."

A lump came into my throat. Tyler Dervish. Maybe it wasn't him. There could be two guys in Halifax with the same name. It was possible.

"What's his age?"

"Hang on a sec. Cops gave me the DOB. Yeah, he'd be, let's see...Nineteen."

"Nineteen."

"Yeah."

Shit. Tyler Dervish. "There was a kid at my school, he dropped out a couple of years ago but he still hung around. He was the guy kids went to when they wanted to party, you know?"

"What was he selling? E? Oxy? Coke? Weed?"

"I don't know, Tenzen. Maybe all that stuff."

"Sounds like a bush party gone wrong."

"Yeah. Maybe." I leaned against the rail with the nausea churning in my gut. He must've been beaten to a pulp, based on the way Phil and Chuck described the cabin. Unless maybe he was the perpetrator. But Tyler? That little runt?

"Is he dead?"

"Cops haven't found a body. That's all I could get from my sources. You got a number for this Tyler kid?"

"Come on Tenzen. That's not my scene. You know that."

"Right. Sorry kid. Any idea where I can find him?"

"He used to hang out in the smokers' corner of the schoolyard. But since school's out...Maybe try the mall."

"Right."

"Get me off this boat, and I'll come help you."

"Sorry. Like I said. Boss' orders."

The boat lurched, throwing me sideways. A cloud of diesel fumes belched from the stern. By the time I got back on the phone, Tenzen had hung up. I swore and stuffed the phone back in my pocket. So much for my last chance at escape. The engine chugged and sputtered as the boat maneuvered away from the wharf.

My Firefly looked lonely in the parking lot, and I hoped no idiot kid would break in and steal my cassette tapes, thinking they were some kind of retro-hip collector's item. On the wharf, Doctor Wallis strode slowly away, the trench coat flapping around his legs. Reaching his car, he turned and raised his hand in a farewell gesture—an ashen figure against a gray backdrop of asphalt and fog.

Four

We spent the morning motoring up the coast under a dull gray sky. There was nothing much to do and nothing much to see, so besides fending off Ernest's attempts to engage me in left-wing political discussion, I passed most of my time leaning on the railing, staring at the water, and pulling my phone out of my pocket every ten minutes in hope that we'd miraculously come within range of a cell tower. It was eating away at me, not knowing what was happening with my story. Had the cops found Tyler? Was he alive or dead? And what about this guy, Hermenegilde Chiasson, the one who owned the property with the bloody shack? Had Tenzen managed to track him down? I wore my battery down to ten percent in the fruitless search for a cell signal before I finally abandoned hope and, succumbing to the previous night's sleep deprivation, climbed down to the galley to take a nap.

I woke to the sound of pots clanging and a cloud of herb-scented steam filling the kitchen. Ms. Cameron was standing in front of the stove, noisily pouring a bag full of something into a huge pot of boiling water.

"Mussels," she said.

"Mmmm." I ran a hand through my frowsy hair. "What time is it?"

"About six. Sorry for waking you. You looked like you were out cold."

"It's okay. Where are we?"

"The Eastern Islands. Go on up on deck and have a look. And tell Ernest dinner will be ready in ten minutes."

I found Ernest on deck, leaning against the railing and admiring the scenery, such as it was.

The Eastern Islands turned out to be a chain of scrubby outcrops, strung out a few miles from the coast. It didn't look like there was anyone around, but a falling-down wooden house on the island we were passing indicated that someone had lived there, once.

"Dinner's in ten," I told Ernest, aiming for a neutral conversation-opener.

"It's a travesty," Ernest replied. Neutral conversation wasn't his thing.

"Dinner?" It seemed like a harsh judgment, considering that Ms. Cameron hadn't even finished cooking.

"No, this." He swept his hand toward the abandoned house.

"What about it?"

"Fishermen used to live around here, on all these islands. One of my grand-uncles did. Then the factory trawlers took all the fish and no one could make a living, so they had to move to the mainland. It was a cultural genocide."

"Right," I said. Those old fishermen were probably the same guys you saw playing darts in every Legion Hall in rural Nova Scotia. I wasn't sure that qualified as cultural genocide—unless being bored to death counted.

Ernest was warming up to his topic, with a long-winded exposé on the sufferings of old-time fishermen, their stoic wives and illiterate kids, when, mercifully, he was interrupted by Ms. Cameron calling us for supper.

The galley was filled with a warm, savory smell and it almost felt homey, despite the odd company and the unatmospheric lighting provided by the single bare bulb that hung above the table. I slid on to my bench, crumpling my sleeping bag into a corner, just as Ms. Cameron set the pot of mussels down on a hot plate in the middle of the table. She ladled some into my bowl then turned to serve Ernest.

He barricaded his plate with both hands.

"I'm a vegetarian."

Of course.

"A mussel isn't exactly a highly evolved life form," said Ms. Cameron. "It's not like a cow. Or even a chicken."

"I don't eat animals. A mussel is an animal."

"In terms of consciousness there's probably not much difference between a mussel and a carrot," Ms. Cameron observed philosophically.

"A carrot is a vegetable."

"Seems a bit hard on the carrot." She shrugged and ladled out some mussels for herself. "There's bread and peanut butter in the cupboard, if you want to make toast."

I ate a few mussels—chewy and salty, flavored with rosemary the same way my Gram made them—and started to feel guilty about how I hadn't exactly been brimming over with enthusiasm for Ms. Cameron's expedition. After all, she was trying to do me a favor and, even though it was misguided, she was being really nice about it. That's what happens when people feed you—it makes you feel warm and fuzzy toward them. There's probably a biological explanation for it, which I would have known if I hadn't skipped so many of Ms. Cameron's classes.

By the second plate of mussels I figured I might as well resign myself to the fact that I'd been reassigned from gritty girl cop reporter to newsroom science geek.

"So, what's so special about this turtle we're going to see?" I asked.

"I'm not sure yet," Ms. Cameron said. "It's more of a hunch than anything else. I caught a glimpse of it and...it was unusual. Really unusual."

"You mean, there's not usually turtles around here?"

Ernest snorted at my ignorance. Ms. Cameron shot him a reproachful look.

"Oh, there's leatherback sea turtles," she said. "They migrate along the Eastern Seaboard. You'll see them up the coast all the way to Cape Breton, and sometimes as far as Newfoundland. But this one looked different."

"How?"

"Well, a leatherback has a flat, greenish, leathery-looking shell. This one had more of a rounded shell, and some different markings. And it was really big."

"A monster sea turtle," I said, thinking headlines.

"I'm not sure I'd say that."

"Show her the photos," said Ernest.

Ms. Cameron went to her cabin and returned with a couple of fuzzy snapshots, about the quality of the latest Loch Ness Monster pics. You could see a dark blob sticking up out of the water that might be a head, and a bigger dark blob that might possibly be a body.

"Definitely a monster turtle," I said. "Either that, or it's the Abominable Snowman, doing the backstroke."

"Very funny, Hayley." Ms. Cameron pocketed the photos. "It may be a rare species. In any case, we've got a proper boat now and some proper equipment, and with any luck we'll be able to get a transmitter on to it, and find out more about it."

We talked logistics for a while, then washed the dishes and cleaned up the galley. Ms. Cameron turned in early and Ernest went on deck to commune with Nature. I figured that Nature didn't need my company, so I sat down on my bunk and wasted the last ten percent of my cell phone battery trying to reach the outside world. No luck. Alexisonfire was playing a gig in Halifax that night and some of my friends were going, but I couldn't even follow their tweets.

Finally giving up on the prospect of making contact with civilization, I wriggled into my sleeping bag and managed to squirm out of my bra and cargo pants. I was turning over to get comfortable, when I saw that Ernest had reentered the galley.

He was standing beside his bunk, peeling his shirt off.

"Just hold it right there," I said.

I wasn't into the teenage dating scene to begin with, but even if I had been, I would have run screaming in horror from the prospect of witnessing Ernest in the raw.

"The human body is nothing to be ashamed of Hayley," Ernest said. He finished stripping off his shirt, revealing a skinny white torso where a few pallid chest hairs sprouted.

"If you take your pants off I'll spray you with the fire extinguisher," I said. Suddenly, I'd gained a new appreciation of the need to keep emergency gear close at hand.

"I wasn't going to. Jeez, you're really repressed, Hayley."

"Keep your pants on, Ernest. I'm serious. And turn off the light."

Ernest reached over and switched off the light, plunging the cabin into pitch blackness.

If things went on like this, it was going to be a long and unappealing summer.

Five

The next day, Ms. Cameron decided we should poke around near a speck on the map called Black Duck Island. She said it was a popular place to see leatherback turtles, so maybe this strange turtle would be hanging out with them, eating jellyfish or doing whatever turtles do. We cruised around for a few hours with binoculars glued to our faces, but didn't see anything beyond a lot of seals and seabirds, so at last we weighed anchor in a sheltered bay. Ms. Cameron killed some time giving us scuba diving lessons, but apart from that, the assignment seemed about as washed-up as a beached whale.

Black Duck Island was the kind of place where some entrepreneur could have built a yuppie eco-lodge, if only he could have airlifted it fifty latitude degrees due south and plopped it in the sunny Carribean. Its main feature was a sandy beach that curved in a long crescent, forming the shoreline of a sheltered bay. The beach was bounded by a rocky bluff, about twenty feet high, that protected it from the wind sweeping over the rest of the island. Near the bluff, the sand was strewn with driftwood logs and boulders, but down by the shoreline it was washed clean and smooth. It was a shame for all that picturesqueness to go to waste, freezing its rocks off here in the North Atlantic.

After the scuba lessons, I finally put on my sweater and oil slicker. It was mid-afternoon, drizzly, overcast. The boat creaked as it rocked on the bay. From somewhere on the island came the high chirrup-chirrup of a shorebird. Ms. Cameron was leaning over the starboard rail, peering out with binoculars over the water. Leaning beside her was Ernest. The kid was turning out to be as irritating as a poison ivy rash. He'd changed out of his wetsuit back into his usual hemp pants, and on top, the latest in a rotation of t-shirts urging people to save the world in ten words or less. This one said, "Extinct Is Forever" above a picture of a sad-eyed panda bear. Ernest smelled like he was boycotting the multinational underarm deodorant industry. I found a place to stand upwind of him and spent a few minutes staring out at the water.

"When do you think this turtle's going to show up?" I said.

"Patience, Hayley. Fieldwork takes time," said Ms. Cameron.

"We've been here for two days," I said. "I have other stories I could be chasing."

"It's not just about your newspaper story," she answered. "I'm expecting a full, written report from each of you. You'll need it to graduate."

I looked over at Ernest.

"Did he fail the final, too?" Somehow, I'd assumed he'd come on the trip as a kind of enrichment activity, maybe to bolster his credentials for university applications. He didn't seem like the type to fail a biology class.

"I didn't fail!" Ernest sounded indignant. He was good at "indignant." He also had "wounded" and "self-righteous" down pat.

"You skipped it?"

"I didn't skip!"

"Ernest had an ethical objection to the frog dissection," Ms. Cameron intervened. "I offered him this research project as an alternative assignment."

"Not easy, being green," I commented. I don't think Ernest got it.

The conversation, like search for the sea turtle, had reached a dead end. I turned away but there wasn't far to go on the boat, so I stood at the rail for a while, thinking about the shack on Concession Road 14. The shack with Tyler Dervish's fingerprints in the blood.

It wasn't true, what I'd told Tenzen, that I didn't know how to get in touch with Tyler. My friend Rhea had his phone number. But I didn't want to get Rhea in trouble. Obviously, she didn't want her parents to know she was doing drugs.

Rhea and I had started an all-girl punk band in high school, along with a bass-player named Morwyn. It went okay for the first couple of years. We played at coffeehouses and all-ages dances, and it helped me survive the ordeal of Boredom High, using my drum riffs to drown out the BS of immature guys and backstabbing girls. But in the past year, things had fallen apart as Rhea and Morwyn discovered the joys of getting trashed after our gigs on vodka and party drugs, supplied by Tyler Dervish. By that time, I was helping Tenzen cover courts and crime, and seeing firsthand all the stupid violence that came out of messing around with drugs and loser guys. So while Rhea and Morwyn partied, I'd go hang out in the newsroom, help the copydeskers proofread the pages, or write some torqued-up headlines for the late-breaking news stories.

I didn't hang out much with Rhea these days, though I still thought of her as my friend. I would've given anything at that point to be able to talk to her—not just to ask her what she knew, but to find out how she was dealing with Tyler's disappearance. Maybe his death.

When I'd had enough of staring at the ocean, I decided to go up to the pilothouse, to see if I could get Captain Gil to tell me his life story. One of the things I'd learned as a reporter was, if you can't get any information, at least get some color. It pads your story and lets you spin a few threadbare facts into twelve inches of copy.

Captain Gil was chewing a toothpick and talking on the radio when I came in, running the French language through the meat-grinder of his Acadian accent.

"*Ouais. Rien. Bon, ben, c'est ton affaire à toi. Bye.*"

He hung up the radio mouthpiece, turned to me, and grunted. I took that as the closest thing to a conversation-opener I was going to get.

"I'm wondering about your life story, Captain." I made myself comfortable on a vinyl-padded bench and pulled my notepad from an inside pocket of my oil slicker. "For my article in the paper."

"Don't matter what I tell you. Papers always get it wrong," Gil growled.

He looked at me like I should have asked permission before plunking myself down in his pilothouse, but I ignored it, along with his low opinion of my trade.

"Whereabouts are you from?" I asked.

"Don't matter, now," he said.

"Big family?"

"Big enough."

"You grew up fishing?" I asked.

"What else?" he shrugged.

"Tough way to make a living," I said, trying the sympathetic-listener gambit.

"Government bought out my license, *hostie*." He shifted his toothpick to the edge of his mouth and leaned forward. "You write this in your goddamn paper: Government sends someone up to my place, tells me 'Don't go fishing no more 'cause there ain't no fish.' I says to him, 'If there ain't no fish, how come you still got a job? You're a fisheries manager, ain't you? How can you manage what ain't there?' Fella's still got his job, far's I know. That's government for you, *tabernac*."

Captain Gil leaned back in his chair, crossed his arms, and shifted the toothpick to the front of his mouth.

"How did you get involved in this research with Ms. Cameron?" I asked.

Captain Gil shrugged.

"I guess you have to make a living somehow," I prompted him. This guy was more tight-lipped than a clam on Krazy Glue. "What do you do mostly? Sport fishing? Tourism?"

"Anything what-for they need a man and a boat," he muttered.

"What's the story behind boat's name? The *Magdelaine*?" I was grasping at straws. Maybe he was devoutly religious. Mary Magdalene, and all that. This would appeal to the older generation of readers who were our most loyal subscribers.

"That was my grandmother. Same name as my grandfather's boat," Captain Gil said.

"He was a fisherman?"

"Made more money running rum. Prohibition times, it was."

"Outsmarted the government, eh?" I said, hoping to hit on the one topic that would make Captain Gil open his mouth.

"That's right," said the Captain.

"Ran it from St. Pierre to the mainland?" I guessed. Everyone knew that during Prohibition, the two tiny islands of St. Pierre and Miquelon had done a booming business, selling alcohol to Canadian and American rum-runners. Liquor was legal on the islands because even though they lay off the east coast of Canada, they belonged to France, a leftover from the old colonial days.

"Never brought it to the mainland. That's how he tricked the government," said Captain Gil. "Left the bottles in the lobster traps, out at sea. Later on, the boys come out and pulled up their traps, and *voila*—that's how they got their deliveries."

"Smart," I said, getting the quotes down on my notepad. It had nothing to do with marine biology research, but it was the kind of local color our readers lapped up.

"Government never caught him. He went down in a storm in 1931." Gil concluded the story with his version of a happy ending, crossed his arms and moved the toothpick to the front of his mouth again. I sensed I wasn't going to get any more stories out of him today.

"Just let me get your name, Captain."

He shrugged.

"Captain Gil."

"I need your full name for the paper," I explained.

"Don't want my name in no newspaper."

It was pointless to persist, and I was thinking that I could probably dig up his name in some fishing vessel registry back in Halifax, when I heard a shout from below. I looked down to see Ernest pointing out over the rail.

"Did you see it?" he yelled, gesturing toward the point of land at the far tip of the bay.

I turned my camera toward the point and adjusted the zoom lens, scanning the water. It was hard to make out anything distinct. The sea was choppy, rolling and breaking into white surf against the rocks. For a second, I thought I saw something poke above the waves—the head of some creature, it might have been, though I couldn't tell exactly what.

"Did you see it?" Ms. Cameron shouted.

"My zoom lens isn't strong enough."

"Use binocs."

I slung the camera to my back and grabbed the pair of binoculars that was hanging from a hook in the pilothouse. I twiddled the knob until the point leapt into focus, startlingly close through the powerful lenses. I could see the texture of the rocks and the fine white fans of spray as the waves broke against the point.

Something jutted out of the water—something dark, shaped like a long, broad blade. A fin, it might have been, or a flipper.

"What was that?"

"Keep watching!"

I fixed my binoculars on the spot. For long moments, nothing—just the waves beating against the rock. Then, something poked above the surface. A head. Yellow eyes staring out through mottled, leathery skin. The head was reptilian, shaped like a giant snake's. As quickly as it had appeared, the head disappeared again.

Please, God, let it be the turtle.

I clambered down the ladder from the pilothouse to join Ernest and Ms. Cameron on deck.

"Is that it?"

"That's it! That's it! I saw it!" Ernest was carrying on like we'd just tracked down the Loch Ness Monster.

A rough guffaw came from behind us and we turned to see Captain Gil leaning out the door of the pilothouse.

"That what you're on about? That's nothing but an old leatherback," he scoffed.

"It wasn't a leatherback!" Ernest's voice was shrill and self-righteous. "I saw it!"

"Right, I don't know nothing," Captain Gil shrugged. "I just been fishing thirty-five years, that's all."

"We need to get a closer look," said Ms. Cameron.

"Water's rough out there. Good chance of smashing against them rocks," Captain Gil predicted with his usual sunny attitude.

"We'll have to see how far we can get. Hayley, could you go below and get the case that Dr. Wallis brought? It's in my cabin."

"Yeah," I said. I'd need an extra battery for my camera, too, just in case. Dad wanted a monster turtle photo. Dad was going to get a monster turtle photo.

I climbed down the ladder into the galley, ducking my head beneath the beam that separated the cooking area from the eating area. As I did, I caught sight of a faded rectangle of paper, taped in a corner near the radio set. The words "Operating License" stood out in bold type. I stopped, and took a step toward it. If Captain Gil wouldn't give me his full name, I could get it off his operating license I thought, gloating a little over my chance to outsmart the old codger.

I pulled out my pen out of my back pocket. Salt air had turned the paper crisp and bleached its original bureaucratic yellow to off-white. In the form's appropriate box, Captain Gil's full, legal name stood in faded black letters:

Hermenegilde Chiasson.

Six

I ditched Dr. Wallis' case at Ms. Cameron's feet and clambered up the metal ladder to the pilothouse.

"*Monsieur Chiasson,*" I said.

Captain Gil turned and stared at me, his eyes dark and heavy as lumps of unrefined metal. He grunted and turned away. I took a step into the pilothouse. The captain stared ahead, ignoring my presence.

It would've made a great profile shot: The gray stubble on his chin, a couple of black hairs sticking out of the bridge of his craggy nose, and the deep wrinkles around his eyes—a face like a bluff, all carved up by the waves. Behind him, the beat-up black box of the boat's radio filled one corner of the frame, and beyond that, the outline of Black Duck Island stood against the sea. Somehow, though, I didn't think Captain Gil was going to go for a photo shoot.

"You own a cabin, don't you? On Concession Road 14?" I said. "It's registered to Hermenegilde Chiasson."

Captain Gil stared out to sea.

"I know the guys who found it the other night," I persisted. "They said it was covered in blood."

"Rough seas around that point," said Captain Gil. "Chasing after a goddamn turtle, *hostie*."

"Do you know a guy named Tyler Dervish?" I asked. An image of Tyler flashed in my mind: his acne-scarred face covered in blood.

"You wanna get wrecked against them rocks, or you wanna let me pilot the boat?" said Captain Gil.

"I want to know what happened in that cabin."

Captain Gil grunted and went back to his deaf-mute impersonation.

"Hayley!" Ms. Cameron called from the deck. "I need you down here, now!"

I shot a last look at Captain Gil but it was obvious he wasn't going to tell me anything. A cabin? Must belong to some other Hermenegilde Chiasson. Common name. Must be hundreds of them in Nova Scotia. The boat pitched and the wind whipped at my cheeks as I climbed down the ladder from the pilothouse. I planted my boots on deck and, hanging on to the ladder with my elbow, zipped up my oil slicker.

"Put on a life jacket, Hayley." Ms. Cameron handed me one from the hatch. I shrugged the thing on over my raincoat, adjusting my camera so that it wasn't stuck underneath, and I could whip it out quickly if we got close enough for a photo. Ernest, already wearing his life vest, was leaning against the rail and squinting through binoculars at the point.

"Do you see it?" I asked

"It was over there. But it dove down."

The sea was getting choppier, the closer the *Magdelaine* got to the point. The waves seemed to be coming from all directions at once: some from the open ocean, some from around the point, some bouncing off the rocks and reflecting back, crashing into the incoming waves and turning the area into a roiling, churning, hazard zone.

We were still a hundred feet off the point when Captain Gil shouted down:

"That's as close as I'll get you."

"Come on," Ms. Cameron said. "Help me launch the *Zodiac*."

The *Zodiac* was an inflatable raft made of tough black rubber, with a flat bottom, a small outboard motor at the back, and cylindrical sides that came together in a point at the bow. It was lashed against the side of the pilothouse. Ernest and I held on to it while Ms. Cameron untied the ropes, and together we maneuvered it to the stern of the *Magdelaine* and shoved it overboard. Ms. Cameron tied it to the rail so it wouldn't drift off. It bobbed on the waves, waiting for us to jump aboard. I couldn't say that it looked very inviting.

Ernest jumped in, lost his footing and ended up on his butt in the bottom. Ms. Cameron helped me down next. Then she took her place in the stern, cast off from the *Magdelaine*, and revved up the outboard motor.

In the few seconds it had taken her to get the motor going, we'd drifted closer to the rocky point. I didn't like the feeling of getting sucked toward it. All we had to do was get caught on the crest of the wrong wave and it would throw us at the rockface, like a drunk smashing a beer bottle against the wall in a bar-fight.

Ms. Cameron must've been thinking the same thing, because she turned the *Zodiac* away from the point and fought against the current to take us further from the rocks. Salt spray lashed my face and hands. The crests of the waves smashed against our bow and we hit the troughs like massive potholes, bouncing and jolting us like we were in a jeep on a rutted dirt road. Ernest knelt in the bottom of the boat, leaning over the side with his elbows propped up and his eyes glued to his binoculars. How he expected to see anything as we lurched from crest to trough was beyond me.

"This is crazy!" I shouted. The wind snatched my voice and buried it under the noise of crashing waves and outboard motor. I grabbed Ms. Cameron's arm and shouted in her face. "This is crazy!"

"Hang on, Hayley!" she shouted.

A wave hit us broadside. I lost my footing, fell and collided with Ernest in a tangle of limbs, a bruising thud of soft tissue and bone. A wave hit us from the other side and we both were tossed backwards, sputtering in the cold salt water that sloshed in the bottom of the *Zodiac*. The rocky point loomed much too near, the sound of the surf much too loud, sucking and roaring against the point.

"Bail!" Ms. Cameron shouted. "Bail!"

Another wave broke over the side of the *Zodiac*. My jeans were soaked. I knelt in the water, searching for a bailer. There it was: a bright orange plastic bucket, strapped under the seat. I ripped open the strap and started scooping water.

A wave picked us up. The boat rose like a rickety amusement-park ride. My stomach heaved. We dropped like a stone into the trough. Another wave grabbed us, flung us forward. Jagged rocks hurtled toward us. I screamed. Somehow, we skimmed sideways along the crest of the wave and with a sudden drop we were back in calm water, on the sheltered side of the point.

I stumbled on my knees to the side of the boat and dry-heaved into the ocean.

"Are you okay, Hayley?"

I didn't answer but lay slumped on my stomach over the side of the boat, my cheek pressed to the black rubber that smelled of car tires.

"We've got to go back! We've got to try again!" Ernest insisted, voice high-pitched like a bratty child.

"Shut up!" I covered my head with my arms. "Shutup, shutup, shutup, shutup, shutup…"

"It's okay, Hayley," Ms. Cameron broke in. "We're not going back out there. It's too dangerous. Besides, even if we got close, we couldn't attach the transmitter. Not in that swell. How about I take you ashore instead?"

"Yes," I mumbled. "Yes. Please."

"We can camp on the point tonight," Ms. Cameron said. "Ernest and I will go back to the *Magdelaine* and pick up the gear."

I didn't argue. I wouldn't have argued if she'd suggested telling ghost stories and singing campfire songs, as long as I didn't have to spend another minute on board a boat.

She dropped me off at the beach and I lay on the sand, trying to soak up some warmth from the late-afternoon sun, while the solid ground still seemed to tilt and rock beneath me.

Seven

Five a.m. dawned cold and lumpy in my Canadian Tire sleeping bag. I tossed and turned, but the ground didn't get any softer, so I crawled out of my tent to see if I could revive the dregs of last night's campfire.

Two other tents hulked silently in the juniper behind me, where Ernest and Ms. Cameron lay sleeping. In front of me, the land jutted to a point, where a blackened circle of rocks marked our extinct campfire. I scuffed together some of the half-charred pieces of driftwood with the toes of my combat boots, added an empty cardboard cracker-box, and struck a match. I'd forgotten to bring a supply of Diet Coke on the trip, but last night's tin coffeepot was still half-full, so I set it on one of the rocks by the campfire and walked around, waiting for it to warm up. Even in my dorky Fair Isle sweater, it was too cold to sit still.

The beach of Black Duck Island lay below a fifteen-foot drop to my right; the ocean a colder, more dangerous, fifteen-foot drop to my left. Waves sloshed against the rocks. A whippoorwill called annoyingly from a hidden location. In the west, a crescent moon slowly petered out, while in the east the sky turned from black to washed-out blue. Soon the scenery would be bathed in that rosy-dawn glow that turned hardcore news photographers into mushy-hearted romantics. I thought about dragging my camera out of my tent and firing off a few shots of the scenery, but artsy pics of the Scotian coast weren't going to get me off this godforsaken voyage. I needed the monster sea turtle.

Way out at sea, the lights of the cargo ships moved slowly, plying the trade routes between Europe and the Eastern Seaboard. They were probably crammed to the brim with high-tech communications equipment, and I couldn't even get a cell signal to call the newsroom.

I wandered back to the campfire, poured myself a cup of coffee and loaded it with sugar from a plastic container. I took a swig; it tasted like warm, flat Diet Coke, laced with a shot of Drano. Why did anyone drink this stuff? I added more sugar and stared out at the sea.

What was the deal with Captain Gil, a.k.a. Hermenegilde Chiasson? He owned the cabin, that was for sure, but what connection could the grizzled old fisherman have to Tyler Dervish?

Maybe there was no connection. It could've been a bush party, like Tenzen said. A bunch of kids found the cabin and broke into it, maybe earlier on prom night, before Phil and Chuck stumbled on the place. Someone was drunk or high on something, some kind of fight broke out. Maybe Tyler wasn't even dead. Maybe he just got hurt really bad, and everyone cleared out when they realized things had gone too far. But wouldn't Phil and Chuck have noticed if it looked like the aftermath of a party? Empty beer and liquor bottles strewn around—they hadn't mentioned any of that.

So maybe Tyler was there partying with some friends and Captain Gil walked in on them. Maybe there was a fight and the kids ended up taking off. Or maybe Gil had a gun—it was a hunt camp after all—and when he found the kids in his cabin he...Would he do that? Shoot a bunch of kids in cold blood for breaking into his cabin?

Something rustled in the junipers behind me. I whipped around. Ernest.

"Hi," he said—an unusually friendly opening—and came to sit on a log beside the campfire.

An odor of wet sheep and unwashed armpits wafted from his hand-knit poncho, mixed with the tang of citronella, which he claimed was a natural alternative to chemically based insect repellants. Based on the red welts on his arms and hands, I guessed the mosquitoes weren't buying it. I stuck my nose into my coffee cup and inhaled.

"It's early," I said.

"I always get up early," he said. "Your biological clock is naturally synchronized to the cycles of the sun, you know."

I shrugged. My biological clock was naturally synchronized to Diet Coke and the night shift, but I didn't feel like arguing with him.

"Have you seen it?" he asked.

"The turtle? No."

Ernest stood up and walked to the edge of the point. He peered into the semi-darkness for a while then turned around and came back to the fire.

"It's out there. I can feel it," he said.

I shrugged again. If Ernest wanted to believe he had a psychic connection to a marine reptile, who was I to bring rationality into the conversation?

Ernest picked up a stick and stirred the fire. He pointed the glowing end at me.

"You don't like me," he said.

"It's not a singles cruise, Ernest. It's a biology trip. What difference does it make?"

He sat down on a log and poked the fire some more.

"Girls don't like me."

He picked up a handful of pebbles and started pelting them glumly at the fire. When he ran out of pebbles, he lifted his head and gave me a searching look, like maybe I had some advice to offer. It was hard to know where to start.

"You could get a haircut," I said.

"Don't be so superficial, Hayley."

"Girls are superficial, Ernest." A sad truth, but someone had to break it to him. "If you've got an extra buck, you could get some of those disposable shaving-razors. Six for ninety-nine cents at Shoppers Drug Mart."

"Oh, shut up."

"You asked for my advice."

"Well, what do you like in a guy, then?" He stared at me, eyes bulging from his pubescent face. All I could think of was Constable Alex Turpin, the way he tucked my business card into his breast pocket, like it was a secret between us. *"Pleasure..."*

I shrugged. "I'm not into the dating scene."

"Why not?"

"Because it's screwed up."

"What do you mean it's screwed up?" said Ernest.

"I mean..." I shook my head, trying to think how to explain it. Did Ernest even have any experience of the dating scene? Or was he just a lonely tree-hugger who'd never kissed anything without bark and branches? "I mean, guys just aren't nice anymore."

"What do you mean? I'm nice." He sounded hurt.

"I mean, they rush things too much. They're too aggressive."

"I'm not aggressive."

"You took your shirt off right in front of me, Ernest."

"I wasn't trying to come on to you! Human nudity is a natural..."

"Okay, okay!" The thought of Ernest in his natural human nudity was too much to stomach before breakfast. Anytime, actually.

"I still don't understand what you're talking about," Ernest said.

"Listen. You go to a club, or a party, and you're out there dancing, and suddenly a guy you don't even know comes up behind you and starts groping you. I mean, when did that become socially acceptable?"

"It doesn't mean anything," Ernest protested, and something about the tone of his voice suggested that maybe he wasn't entirely innocent.

"You just made my point."

"What point?"

"The point is, that's what guys always say: 'What's the problem, baby? Why are you so uptight? It doesn't mean anything.' And then they expect you to have sex with them because, if it doesn't mean anything, why should you say no?"

"But maybe it doesn't mean anything. It's just a biological function..."

"And maybe it does mean something. The point is, why do guys think that *they* get to decide if it's meaningful or not? When they're not even the ones who are going to get pregnant if something goes wrong."

"You can always get an abortion."

"Oh, yeah, like that's an easy thing to do." Maybe it was easy for some girls, but I was the child of an unwanted teenage pregnancy, and it wasn't so simple for me to think about waltzing into a clinic and getting rid of a baby that shared my same sorry start in life.

Ernest pelted a couple of pebbles into the fire. "Well, what if you really like a guy?"

"That's almost worse."

"Why?"

"Because then you sleep with him, and you put your heart into it, and half the time he doesn't really care, he's just using you. As soon as you get serious about him, he'll turn around and break up, and do the same thing to another girl."

"You really have a hate on for men, Hayley."

"I don't have a hate on for men."

"Maybe you're a lesbian."

"Don't make me laugh."

"It's not a joke. One in ten people are gay, you know."

"Ernest, I can't talk to you about this. If you have girl problems, why don't you talk to your mother?"

"My mother's not around." Ernest lowered his head and stared into the fire.

"Yeah, well mine isn't either." It came out sounding angry, but as soon as I said it, I felt my anger toward him fading. Who'd have thought we'd turn out to have something in common?

"Where's your mom?" he asked.

"She took off."

"Where to?"

"I don't know. I was a baby."

"Oh. Did you ever try to find her?"

"I'm on Facebook," I said. "She can look me up."

"Oh. Yeah, I guess," said Ernest.

We sat there in silence for a bit. I didn't feel like sharing with Ernest any of the tawdry details that I'd gathered from my Gram's whispered comments, or my dad's occasional angry outbursts. How Mom was a drunken party girl. How the only reason I hadn't ended up with fetal alcohol syndrome was because she was too throwing-up sick to drink during the pregnancy. How she couldn't wait to get back to partying once I was born. How she was too immature to take care of a baby. It was all too pointlessly hurtful to talk about, so instead I just sat there, letting the warmth of the coffee cup soak into the skin of my hands while the rest of me felt chilled to the bone.

"My mom's on a commune in PEI," Ernest offered.

"Really? Why don't you live with her?" I said. A commune in PEI sounded right up Ernest's alley.

"I can't. It's women only. She wanted to get away from the threat of the patriarchy."

I looked at Ernest, huddled in his ratty poncho. If he was the best threat the patriarchy could come up with, the patriarchy was definitely losing its edge.

"It's a radical feminist commune," he explained.

I didn't know such a thing existed in the land of *Anne of Green Gables*. Someone should probably alert the Tourism Standards Board.

"When did she leave?" I said.

Ernest picked up another handful of pebbles and pelted them into the fire.

"I was eight," he mumbled. I got the feeling he didn't want to talk about his mom leaving, any more than I did. It was one thing to spew philosophical concepts like 'the patriarchy' and 'radical feminism.' But how did it make an eight-year-old boy feel, when his mom looked him in the eye and told him she was abandoning him to go plant cabbages with a bunch of gal-pals on the Island? It probably blew a big, black hole right into the middle of his life.

"Nice thing, walking out on your family," I said.

"Family is a social construct, Hayley," said Ernest miserably.

"You have kids, you're supposed to take care of them," I said. "That's not a social construct. That's just life."

Ernest threw another pebble in the fire. For once, he had nothing to say. Maybe I should have felt satisfied that I'd won an argument against him, but I didn't. It's not satisfying to win an argument when the other person's in too much pain to argue.

I got up and walked to the edge of the bluff. The morning was clear and calm. The sun had just broken over the horizon, the first rays hitting the long, golden crescent of beach. I was thinking again about getting out my camera, and that's when a saw it: a large, dark shape moving on the sand, high up near the bluffs.

I could see the hulk of a massive body, and four things that looked like flippers sticking out the sides. It was some kind of creature, and it was trapped behind a large driftwood log—probably stranded by the receding tide. It looked like it was trying to get around the log and make its way back to the ocean. I must have let out some kind of a shout, because the next thing I knew, Ernest was standing beside me.

"What is it?"

"I think we found it."

Ernest pulled a pair of binoculars from beneath his poncho.

"The turtle!" he shouted. "The turtle!"

I brushed past him, grabbed my knapsack from my tent and threw my camera and a notepad inside it.

"You get Ms. Cameron," I said as I ducked past Ernest and headed toward the bluff.

"What? Me? What if she's not dressed?"

"Deal with it," I said.

I wasn't about to miss this shot at the photo that would get me off this assignment and back to the city where I belonged.

Eight

A stand of tough little cedar bushes grew sideways over the edge of the bluff. I grabbed a couple by their gnarly trunks and swung myself down so I was facing the cliff, my Fair Isle sweater snagging on the roots. My feet scrabbled around until they found a ledge, but when I let go of the cedars my foothold crumbled and I went slithering and scraping down to the beach. So much for the glamour of adventure journalism.

I picked myself up and looked around. The morning light still had that artsy glow, dewy and pastel-colored. Great for a landscape shot with a tripod and a long exposure, but kind of tricky for photographing anything living and moving. I could use a flash if I had to, but I didn't want to freak the creature out. Who knew if it might attack? If I pumped up the ISO and dialed down the f-stop, maybe I could capture it its natural light. It would make for a nicer picture, too. Just in case *National Geographic* ever called, asking for a reprint.

In any case, the animal was too far away to start shooting now. I left my camera tucked in my backpack and started scrambling across the boulders and driftwood logs that cluttered the beach above the high-tide mark. It was hard to keep an eye on the creature with all the obstacles in the way, so I didn't get a good look at it until I reached a rock about ten feet away from the big, salt-bleached log that held it stranded in the receding tide.

If dad wanted an exotic monster of the deep, we'd found one, all right. Its shell looked like a boulder: it must have been five feet across, and it would have come up to my shoulder, if I'd felt like going to measure myself against it. It was a mottled gray-green color, encrusted with mollusks and barnacles, and marked with a yellow-orange starburst that started in the center of the dome and radiated out to the edges. Four huge, oar-like flippers, covered in leathery-brown hide, stuck out from beneath the shell.

The turtle was making good progress around the log, dragging itself through the sand with a rowing motion of its flippers. I set my backpack on a rock and dug out my camera, just as the shadow of the bluffs drew back and the first rays of sun touched the creature. I fired off a few shots. I had just enough light to work without a flash, but I needed to get around front, where I could see the thing's face.

I crept over to another boulder about ten feet further down the beach and looked out. The turtle's head was enormous, the size of a ten-gallon bucket, with mottled brown-green hide pulled taught over a bony skull, and yellow eyes peering out above a toothless, reptilian mouth. Its face looked ancient, Yoda-like, as though at any moment it might croak out some deep and cryptic aphorism on the Meaning of Life.

I raised my camera and fired off a few dozen shots. Zoomed in tight on the turtle's face. Zoomed out for a wider angle. I would have given a good chunk of change for a fish-eye lens; that was the only thing that could have captured its whole head and body close-up, in one frame. As it was, I had to make the best of my second-rate gear.

What I really needed was something to give perspective, to show how big the turtle really was. I looked around, and that was when I saw Ernest and Ms. Cameron, crouching behind a boulder a few feet away. Ms. Cameron was kneeling in the sand, opening the case that Dr. Wallis had given her.

"Ernest!" I hissed. "Get over there and stand next to it. I need a picture of you both."

"We're not here for a photo-op, Hayley!" he hissed back. I shrugged. It was worth a try.

By now, the turtle had managed to crawl around the log and was starting to head toward the ocean. If I climbed on to the log, I could get a picture of it from above. I ducked out from behind my boulder and dodged across the sand.

"Hayley!" Ms. Cameron hissed. I pretended not to hear her. Just a few more shots, then I'd go back and help out with the GPS gear—though how she expected to get a radio-tag on this monster, I had no idea.

I stood up on the log, braced one foot against the stub of a thick branch, and wedged the other into a hollow. I raised my camera and zoomed out to capture the turtle's entire body in one, wide-angled frame. The thing was still too big: I couldn't help cutting off the tips of the flippers. I crouched down to get a different angle, fired a few shots, then I heard Ms. Cameron's voice shouting:

"For God's sake Ernest, get out of the way!"

I turned toward their voices. Ms. Cameron was still standing behind the boulder, holding something that looked like a power drill. Ernest was planted in front of her, barring her way and waving his arms like a demented crossing-guard.

"Ernest, for Christ's sake! I'm not going to hurt it!" she shouted.

"I can't let you do it!" Ernest shouted back. "It's not right!"

Jesus, Ernest. If he screwed this up now when I was so close to getting my story, I'd throttle him.

Ms. Cameron tried to step around him, but he deked left and stopped her. She moved the other way, and he deked to the right. Ms. Cameron faked to the right, vaulted onto the boulder and dropped down on the other side. Fancy move, for a science teacher. Ernest whirled, dodged around the boulder, and leapt at her. He grabbed her knees in a football tackle and brought her thudding to the sand.

"Ernest!" I shouted. Was the guy deranged? I stuffed my camera in my backpack and by the time I turned around again, he was lying on top of Ms Cameron, trying to wrench the drill out of her hand. I grabbed him by the shoulders and pried him off the teacher just as he'd managed to rip the drill out of her grasp.

He spun around, vaulted over a log, and went sprinting down the beach.

"Ernest!" Ms. Cameron shouted. She tried to stand up but cried out in pain and collapsed, clutching her ankle.

"Are you okay?"

"Get him! Get the drill, Hayley!"

"Ernest!" I shouted, and took off after the rogue agent of the Animal Liberation Front.

He didn't look back, dashing toward the ocean, like a football player on a clear run for the endzone. I caught up to him ten feet before he reached the shoreline, and threw a diving tackle that brought him down with a thud.

"Hayley, get off of me! Are you crazy?"

"Let go of that drill!"

"Never!"

I climbed on top of him and grabbed his wrists, and we went tussling over the sand like a deranged parody of a teenage beach movie. His poncho smothered my face with the stench of sweat and feral llama. Our legs tangled together. His chest pressed against me. I twisted my body to keep his pelvis away; the last thing I wanted was to feel Ernest's groin pressed against mine. His pulse throbbed fast beneath my fingers; his wiry muscles strained to break away. I held my grip, digging my fingernails into his wrists.

"Ernest," I jerked my head to free my face from the poncho. "If you don't let go of that drill, so help me God, I'm going to bite you."

"You wouldn't…do that," Ernest panted back.

I sunk my teeth into his wrist. It felt like biting into a bony chicken-wing. Ernest let out a shriek and dropped the drill with a thud. I threw him off me and grabbed it.

"Ms. Cameron!" I ran toward her. She was lying on the sand, holding her ankle.

"No, Haley! Go, catch it!" she shouted.

She pointed down the beach. The sea turtle had nearly reached the ocean. I changed course, running beside the track in the sand made by the creature's dragging underbelly. Ernest was on his feet and running after me. I tried to speed up, but couldn't get any traction on the soft, shifting sand. I reached the water's edge just in time to see the enormous creature push off with its strong back flippers, and disappear into the waves.

Ms. Cameron came limping up beside me. Her shoulders slumped.

"I'm sorry," I said.

"It's not your fault, Hayley."

Ernest caught up to us, panting.

"You idiot! What did you do that for?" I shouted. It was all I could do to stop myself from punching him out.

"She was going to drill a hole! In its shell!"

"So what?"

"So, a turtle has nerves, you know. In its shell! How would you like it if someone just came along and drilled a hole in you?"

"I've already explained: it's no more harmful than piercing your earlobe." Ms. Cameron's voice was tight with controlled anger. She turned to me to explain.

"We needed the hole to tether the transmitter to the turtle. The transmitter sends location data to a satellite, which allows us to track the turtle's movements on an encoded website. I've activated the transmitter. All we needed to do was attach it to the turtle."

"And our job would've been done," I said.

Ms. Cameron nodded.

"And we could've gone home."

"Yes, I told Dr. Wallis we'd return and give him an update."

"Ernest, you stupid..."

"I couldn't let her do it!" he broke in. "There's other ways that are way more humane! That's what I was trying to tell you, if you'd listened to me. I saw in this one nature documentary where they were attaching satellite transmitters to turtles with a little harness, like a backpack. We could..."

"Shut up, Ernest," I said.

Ms. Cameron didn't say anything. She took the drill from my hand and started limping back to where she'd left the case with the rest of Dr. Wallis' equipment.

"You kids have ten minutes to get your things together," she said over her shoulder. "Ernest, I'm taking you to the *Magdelaine*. Hayley, you and I are going out to look for it."

Fabulous. Yet more adventures in the deep blue sea, when all I wanted was to get back to the newsroom and chase drug dealers.

Nine

The *Zodiac* scudded through the calm bay as Ms. Cameron steered toward the *Magdelaine*. Ernest sat opposite me. He looked hurt and defiant: defiant, because he was sure he'd done the right thing, and hurt because no one appreciated him for it. That was the problem with Ernest. He was the kind of guy who gave "doing the right thing" a bad name.

I clutched my camera tight beneath my oil slicker. The last thing I needed was for Ernest to grab it and fling it into the briny deep before I could download the turtle pics. He probably thought I'd invaded the turtle's privacy by taking its picture without a signed consent waiver—not to mention the ethics of exploiting its image to sell tabloid newspapers.

But Ernest didn't move until Ms. Cameron pulled alongside the *Magdelaine*. He climbed aboard without saying anything. Ms. Cameron didn't say anything either, just pushed off from the side of the boat with an oar and gunned the little outboard motor.

Frankly, I was skeptical of our chances of capturing and tagging the creature. It was too big to haul into the dinghy and, from what I'd seen as it swam away, strong and fast in the water. I couldn't imagine it would just float there like a piece of driftwood while we pulled up alongside and drilled a hole in its shell. I didn't say any of that to Ms. Cameron, though. She looked like she didn't want to hear any back talk from anyone.

We searched for three hours, until the sea began to get choppy and my eyes burned from the glare of the sun off the waves. I was feeling seasick by the time we got back to the *Magdelaine*. Acid churned in my stomach, empty of anything except that cup of early-morning nuclear coffee. Static and a throbbing backbeat filled my brain, like a heavy-metal band on a badly tuned radio.

"You go aboard. Get something to eat and some rest, Hayley," Ms. Cameron said. She handed me the case that Dr. Wallis had given her, with the transmitter gear inside. "Put that away somewhere safe. I'm going back to the island. I want to make some sketches and plaster casts of the turtle's tracks on the sand. I'm taking a radio with me, so you can call me if something comes up."

I climbed aboard and headed straight down to the galley. Ernest wasn't there; he must have been somewhere on deck, communing with the Great Outdoors. Personally, I'd had enough of the Great Outdoors, even though the galley, which smelled like the bottom of a dirty laundry hamper, was hardly a better alternative. I opened the storage hatch beneath my bunk and shoved the case with the transmitter gear into a back corner, covering it with a wad of filthy clothes. I wasn't about to give Ernest another opportunity to throw our equipment overboard and sabotage the expedition.

I peeled off my dirty t-shirt and grabbed a fresh one from my duffle bag. Not that it did much good. My skin was covered by a layer of insect repellent and grime. My hair, matted with three-day-old gel, reeked of campfire smoke. A hot shower was a luxury beyond the wildest dreams of the *Magdelaine*.

I closed the storage hatch and wrapped myself in a sleeping bag on the bunk.

It was only noon, but I'd been up since five a.m. and the oblivion of sleep seemed preferable to staying awake and running the risk that Ernest might decide to seek out my company and continue our conversation about animal rights. Or human nudity. Or some equally awkward topic on which we were nearly one hundred percent guaranteed to disagree.

I plumped up my pillow and nestled deeper into the sleeping bag. Of course, Ernest wasn't the only one on board. There was also Captain Gil. It creeped me out to think of going to sleep on the same boat with the Captain, now that I knew he owned the cabin where Tyler had been beaten up and maybe murdered. He knew that I knew. And he knew that I was a reporter. What was to stop him from suffocating me in my sleep and throwing the body overboard? He could claim I'd drowned in a tragic accident. Who could ever prove he was lying?

I shook off the sleeping bag, tiptoed up the ladder and grabbed the hatch-door. One swift tug brought it clunking down. I rammed the bolt shut. Safe. For now. But on the way back to bed, I took the emergency hatchet from its fastening on the wall and hid it under my pillow, just in case.

I'd been asleep for a couple of hours, when I woke to the screeching of Ernest's voice:

"I'm telling you, we have to get over there! They're going to kill her!"

The sleeping bag grabbed at my legs as I struggled to my feet, stumbled up the ladder and fumbled with the bolt.

"Do you want to have blood on your hands?" Ernest shrieked. "Do you want them to get away with murder?"

I unbolted the trapdoor, pushed it open and stuck my head out the hatch. The weather was overcast and gloomy, but there was enough light in the sky for me to guess the time at about mid-afternoon.

"What's going on?" I rubbed my eyes with the palms of my hands.

"Hayley!" Ernest gestured frantically. "You were sleeping! And they're going to kill her! And he's going to let them!"

Ernest jabbed his finger toward Captain Gil. The captain was standing on deck, arms crossed over his chest, feet bolted to the floor.

"Who's going to kill who? What are you talking about?" I hauled myself up on deck, shaking off dreams of Captain Gil as a grim murderer, blasting away at a bunch of scared teenage kids. When I looked at the Captain now, he seemed like nothing more than a grumpy old fisherman. Disgruntled, yes, but who wouldn't be, with Ernest raving and dancing around like a lunatic?

"The turtle, Hayley!"

The turtle. I could've laughed if I wasn't so tired. Me, paranoid about being killed in my sleep, and Ernest still going on about the turtle.

"What about the turtle?" I came to stand beside Ernest at the railing.

"She's over there. I've been watching her. See that fishing boat? If she gets tangled in the net, she'll drown. And Captain Gil won't do anything to save her."

"Local lads got a right to fish," Captain Gil grumbled.

I looked where Ernest was pointing and saw a boat bobbing on the water, just off the point where we'd first spotted the turtle. It outclassed the *Magdelaine* by a mile: sleek lines, a gleaming white hull with a broad, sky-blue stripe, and all sorts of aerials and antennae sticking up from its pilothouse. Looked like the "local lads" had won the lottery.

A fog was starting to gather, not in a rolling bank, but in thin wisps that scudded over the water like ghosts. Along the shoreline of Black Duck Island, bits of fog hung off the scrubby trees and crags. I couldn't see the turtle, but that didn't surprise me. In the water, the thing was practically impossible to spot with the naked eye.

"You sure it's out there?" I said.

Ernest offered me his binocs.

"Look for yourself. I've been watching it for half an hour."

"Half an hour?" I waved away the binocs. "Why didn't you call Ms. Cameron? Do you realize we spent three hours looking for that stupid turtle this morning?"

"I can't do that. She wanted to..."

"Forget it, Ernest." There was no use talking to him. The guy was a total lunatic. I headed back toward the galley.

"Where are you going?"

"To radio Ms. Cameron."

"You can't do that, Hayley!"

"Yes, I can."

"We don't have time. We have to do something. They could catch her any minute. Besides, one of the guys on that boat has a gun."

I stopped halfway down the ladder and climbed back on deck. I grabbed the binocs out of Ernest's hand and leveled them at the boat.

There were two guys on deck: one of them was casting out a net from a winch in the stern; the second was standing beside him, brown hair sticking out beneath a baseball cap. His back was turned to me, and if he had a gun, I couldn't see it. He opened a hatch and disappeared below deck.

"Don't be stupid, Ernest," I said. "People don't go fishing with guns."

"That's what I saw!"

"I'm calling Ms. Cameron."

"Don't!"

I ignored him and went below.

The grogginess had cleared from my mind. I put out a call to Ms. Cameron on the radio and while I waited for her to answer, I tried to figure out what a couple of "local lads" were doing, riding around in a luxury boat. Did they really have a gun, or was that just a product of Ernest's eco-warrior fantasy?

There had been some disputes over fishing licenses around the province lately. The government had cut way back on the amount people were allowed to catch, trying to protect the dwindling stocks of cod and flounder. But the Native communities still had fishing rights guaranteed in their treaties—and that got the other fishermen up in arms, especially since some of *their* families had been fishing on the Scotian coast for four hundred years.

So, maybe these guys were Natives trying to protect their rights. Or maybe they were non-Natives, trying to take what they thought they were owed. That could explain the gun Ernest thought he saw. But it still didn't explain the ritzy boat.

I told Ms. Cameron the gist of it over the radio.

"Sit tight," she said. "I'm coming. Don't do anything till I get there."

I climbed on deck to pass the message on to Ernest, but by the time I got there, he was dressed in a diving suit, squeezing his feet into a pair of swimming flippers. The black neoprene wetsuit on his tall, skinny body made him look like one of those bendable, wire-and-rubber action figures. The Gumby of Greenpeace.

"Ms. Cameron said to wait till she gets here," I said.

He didn't answer. The fog had grown thicker, even in the short time it had taken me to call Ms. Cameron. Now the wisps clung together in solid patches. Between the patches, I could still see bits of the island and the fishing boat, but soon more fog would come to fill in the spaces. Then we'd be lucky to see two feet in front of us.

I raised the binocs again and zeroed in on the bow of the fishing boat. Its name was painted in black letters: *Ferox.* I panned up, but couldn't see anyone on board. The fog was getting thicker by the minute. All that remained of the island was a ghostly outline.

I lowered the binocs and turned back to Ernest. He'd fastened a belt around his waist with a knife in a sheath the size of a dagger. He was fiddling with a compass.

"What's that, your pirate costume?" I asked.

He ignored me.

"One hundred ten degrees east-south-east." Ernest clipped the compass to his belt and started to climb over the side of the boat. I grabbed his arm. It was more muscular than you'd expect from a guy who lived on roots and berries.

"Are you crazy?"

"I know what I'm doing, Hayley. My dad taught me to scuba dive when I was fourteen."

"What are you going out there for?"

"To cut the net."

"Ernest, don't be stupid."

"Saving Nyota isn't stupid, Hayley."

"Nyo-what?"

"I named her Nyota. The turtle. I means "star" in Swahili."

Of course. I should have known.

"I thought you said one of those guys had a gun."

"Yeah, so?"

"So, messing with armed men is stupid, Ernest."

"You don't care, Hayley. You don't care about Nyota or anything. All you care about it getting your dumb newspaper story."

"Yeah, great story," I said. "Armed fishermen kill teenage idiot."

"Shut up, Hayley."

"Just wait a second, would you Ernest?"

He could have broken away from me if he'd wanted to, dropped over the side of the boat and disappeared. He didn't, though. He hung there on the rail, staring at me, and I stared back at him.

It was easy enough for Ernest to play the hero. Not only was he motivated by fanatical zeal, but he actually knew what he was doing around a scuba tank. As for me, the only diving experience I had was the lesson Ms. Cameron had given us the day before. Although it had gone well, I still felt like a rank novice underwater. Still, I couldn't let Ernest take off all by himself. And besides, Ernest was right. Whatever happened out there, it had the makings of a great story.

"Well?" said Ernest.

I didn't know what I was going to say until I opened my mouth and said it:

"I'm coming with you."

Ten

The water closed in around me and with it, a feeling of claustrophobia. I gagged on my scuba mouthpiece, felt panic claw at my throat. *Breathe, Hayley. Calm down and breathe.* I forced myself to inhale slowly, suck the air from the scuba tank—pause, hold the breath in my lungs—exhale it slowly in a stream of bubbles.

Ernest's flippers flashed in front of me. I dove down, following them. A fat fish, hovering over a rock ledge, gaped at me with beady eyes. Seaweed shimmered in the current. Jellyfish parachuted past. Anemones encrusted the seabed, looking more like rocks than living animals. Everything moved in serene slow motion—everything except the schools of tiny silver fish that flashed to and fro. It was like falling into one of those New Age visioning exercises. The only thing missing was the sound of tinkling bells and maybe a gong or two.

Within the dreamy seascape, Ernest moved with purpose. As I followed behind him, the rock ledge gradually fell away and we were surrounded on all sides by nothing but millions of gallons of salt water. I turned to look behind. The hull of the *Magdelaine* had disappeared from sight. I had no idea where the boat or the island lay. Our only means of orientation was

Ernest's compass—an uncertain tool on which to hang our lives.

I'd lost track of time and distance, when Ernest drew alongside me, grabbed my arm, and pointed at something ahead. If we'd been above water, he'd have been shouting in my ear. Ernest, it turned out, was a lot more bearable with the sound turned off.

I followed the line of his gesture and saw, floating amid a school of fish, the massive, gray-green shell of the turtle, marked with an orange starburst. The beast looked, if possible, huger here than it had on land, and far more graceful. It seemed fantastical, that massive shell floating weightlessly; those yellow eyes peering out from its mottled face. It reminded me of those gigantic stone statues of animal gods that you saw in *National Geographic*. It was like a creature from a myth, something that had broken off of the Earth's crust and come to life.

As we came closer, I noticed the lattice of a fishing net separating us from the turtle and from the swarm of fish around it. The net dangled loosely, waving in the current. Ernest grabbed it with one hand, drew his knife and began to hack away at the mesh. The turtle paid no attention. It was busy eating jellyfish.

Twenty feet above us and a little off to the side, a large white shape floated on the surface of the water—obviously, the hull of the fishing boat. Ernest hadn't been working for long when a mechanical, grinding noise rumbled through the water and the net began to draw in and rise up, tightening around its catch.

Ernest clung to the net, slashed at the criss-crossed fibers. The fish, sensing danger and a means of escape, came thronging out through the widening hole. The turtle made no move to evade capture. As the net drew closer to the surface, Ernest became more frantic, reaching toward the giant creature and waving his arms at it—a failed experiment in human-reptile communication.

The net broke the surface of the water. Ernest still clung to it. The crack of a firearm rang out from above. The turtle broke through the net, dove with the force of a cannonball. It skimmed past me so close I could have touched it, but the rushing water pushed me backwards, sending me tumbling into a seething swarm of panicked fish. Fragments of shot pelted through the froth. A red cloud tinted the water. Somewhere in the melee I caught sight of Ernest. I grabbed his arm and pulled him away from the boat. A motor roared. Water churned. I tightened my grip on Ernest's arm, not sure which way was up or down in the chaos of fish and roiling water. The air rasped through my scuba mask. A giant ray winged past. I took a chance and dove after it, dragging Ernest along with me. The ray dove fast and deep. The fish scattered in all directions. One moment we were caught in the turbulence. The next, the tumult dissipated and the ocean around us became dim and calm.

I let go of Ernest's arm. His other arm dangled limp at his side, a ribbon of red streaming out from a spot a few inches below his shoulder. I looked up. The sky glowed at the water's surface. No white shape indicating the hull of a boat. I motioned up and Ernest nodded, so we slowly rose through the quiet sea, exhaling bubbles, giving our bodies time to adjust to the changing pressure. I kept casting my eyes around for the shape of the fishing boat's hull, but there was no sign of it. At last we reached the surface.

Fog. Nothing but fog.

I spat out my mouthpiece.

"Did you get hurt?" I whispered.

"She's free, Hayley! Did you see it? She escaped!"

"Shush, Ernest! What if they're still around?"

I peered into the fog but couldn't see a thing. All I could hear was the shriek of seagulls and the distant moan of a foghorn.

"I did it, Hayley! Nyota's free!"

"That's great, Ernest," I said. "But we've got to get out of here. Are you okay to swim?"

"Why wouldn't I be okay to swim?"

"Your arm. It looks like it got hurt."

Ernest turned his head to look. A faint pink stained the water immediately around his arm. He looked surprised.

"I can't move it," he said.

"Does it hurt?"

"Yeah. Kind of."

Maybe he was in shock. Maybe he was on an adrenaline high. Either way, we needed to get back to the boat.

"I need your compass," I said. I didn't wait for him to pass it to me, but reached over, unclipped it from his belt, and clipped it onto one of the straps of my scuba tank. It was a big, heavy, brass instrument with the Swiss Army logo stamped into it. It felt reassuring—better than some crappy, plastic dollar-store item from a Chinese sweatshop.

I knew enough to line up the bobbing needle with the N on the compass. Anything else went beyond the limit of my skill.

"So that's north," I said. North pointed in exactly one direction: fog. So did South, East, and West. "What do we do next?"

Ernest coughed as a splash of salt water smacked him in the mouth.

"Our line was one hundred ten degrees east-south-east," he said, recovering. "So we want to go…"

"One hundred ten degrees west-north-west?" I guessed.

"No, two hundred ninety degrees west-north-west."

"Huh?" I squinted at the compass.

"Sure," Ernest continued. "Because you add one hundred eighty degrees...But then we should try to compensate for currents and tide...so that would mean..."

"Okay, forget it." The last thing I needed was an orienteering lesson. "We're not going to find the boat anyways. We're probably way off course. Why don't we head for the island? It's a bigger target."

"Yeah, good idea."

"So that would be...where...?"

I peered into the fog, hoping it would part and reveal the island like a Biblical miracle. No such luck.

"North. And a little bit west," Ernest said.

He was happy to be the guy who knew the answers, and if it made him happy, it made me happy. Even with the flippers, my legs were getting tired from treading water. The last thing I needed was to start fighting with the only other human being around.

We put in our scuba mouthpieces and dove again, not deep, but far enough down to avoid the rough chop on the water's surface. I kept hold of the compass, leaving Ernest his one good arm to swim with.

We were still in deep water, with no landmarks anywhere around, no friendly rockshelf with its anemones and seaweeds that would have told us we were close to the island. The vastness of the ocean gave me a shiver that could easily turn to terror. My heart raced. I forced myself to breathe more slowly. I forced myself to focus on keeping the needle lined up with the N on the compass, on following the line that pointed north-north-west. I had to believe the island lay in that direction, and we'd bump into it as long as we kept going. As long as we paced ourselves. As long as we conserved our energy. As long as we had faith, if not in Biblical miracles, then at least in Swiss engineering.

I looked back. Ernest was trailing behind. I slowed my pace to let him catch up. A thin ribbon of red streamed from the wound in his arm. We had nothing to bind it with. I could only hope the wetsuit provided some compression, while the sea water washed it clean. I pointed at it, and Ernest gave me the "okay" sign. I floated there beside him for a few moments, resting, listening to the air being sucked from my scuba tank into my lungs, then escaping out, into the ocean. How much air did we have left?

Time and distance slipped by without landmarks. I tried not to ask myself if we'd accidentally swum past the island. I tried not to question the compass bearing. My feet and fingers grew numb. Weariness seeped into my body. Yet somehow, I felt as though I could keep slogging onward for hours, as long as I didn't need to speed up, or to think. As long as all I needed to do was kick my legs and follow the compass.

I wasn't so sure about Ernest. His face had grown pale and his hands were white. I often had to slow down and wait for him. The ribbon of red, though small and faint, still seeped from the wound in his arm. How much blood had he lost?

The steady rasp of air through the scuba tank gave a pace to my forward motion. I counted to it, riffed off songs in my head to its beat, until finally I inhaled—and choked on emptiness. Nothing left in the tank.

I tapped Ernest on the shoulder and motioned upward. Breaking through the surface, I spat out the mouthpiece. The fog hadn't lifted. It weighed heavy on the black-green water. The foghorn called from somewhere afar. I took a breath and the salty, organic smell made me queasy after the pure air of my scuba tank.

"Tank's empty," I told Ernest. I shrugged it off and let it sink into the depths.

"You can't just dump it," Ernest said. The guy's concern for the environment never ended.

"I'm not carrying an empty tank. God knows how much further we've got to go," I said. I could see he was having trouble treading water with his one good arm. "You should dump yours, too. You can't have much air left."

I checked the gauge on his scuba tank and sure enough, it read just above empty. Ernest didn't fight as I unclipped the buckles and slid the tank off his back. If the sinking of the Titanic hadn't destroyed the marine eco-system, one more piece of jetsam wasn't going to make any difference.

"How do you feel?" I asked him.

"Cold," said Ernest. "Starving."

"Yeah, me too."

My hands were white, my fingernails purple. My legs ached with the effort of keeping my head above water. It seemed to take more energy to stay in one place than to swim forward.

"Ready to keep going?" I asked.

Ernest nodded. I reached for the compass.

It wasn't there.

"Shit. The compass."

"The compass?" Ernest's eyes went blank for a fraction of a second. "The compass? You lost the compass? How could you lose the compass?"

"When I got rid of the air tank…" *I'd clipped it to the harness…*

"The compass? Hayley, the compass? Oh shit. Oh, shit, shit, shit."

"Don't freak out, Ernest." I fought down panic. "It's going to be okay."

"How, Hayley? How is it going to be okay? I don't even know which way we were going."

"The fog'll lift," I said. But it could be hours, days.

"Help!" Ernest shrieked at the top of his lungs. "Ms. Cameron! Captain! Help!"

I started shouting along with him, shouting and panting and pumping my legs to keep afloat. I shouted until my voice went hoarse and the salt spray burned my throat.

Nothing answered but the bellow of the foghorn.

Eleven

My body was a deadweight. Sandbagging me. Dragging me down. Facedown, my limbs dangling numb and heavy in the water. Only my lungs kept me afloat: two living bubbles of air and hope.

I had never been so aware of my lungs. My entire mind was focused on them, as though my brain had left my skull, jumped ship and headed for the pulmonary liferaft. I turned my head sideways. Inhaled. Felt the air buoying my chest. Held my breath. Put my face down. Stayed afloat for one more breath.

I'd learned the trick in some long-ago swim class, a skinny seven-year-old shivering her way through Red Cross certification in an under-heated, over-chlorinated pool. The jellyfish, they called it. If I ever got back to civilization, I was going to phone the Red Cross and tell them it felt nothing like a jellyfish—nothing so floaty and ephemeral. It felt a like lead weights tied to a balloon. And you hoped you could keep the balloon inflated for long enough to stop the lead weights from pulling it down. Down into the immense blackness of the ocean, where you'd drown long before you hit bottom.

Exhale. Feel my lungs deflate, my body start to sink. Turn head. Inhale. Hold breath. Survive. I had no idea if the tide was coming in or going out. If it was coming in, we might get swept ashore on Black Duck Island. If it was going out...but it was best not to think about that.

My head throbbed like a crowded dance bar. The bar where I'd played with Rhea and Morwyn at an all-ages dance last year, one of our best gigs. In the darkness behind my closed eyelids, laser lights strobed and I heard the thrashing soundtrack of "Crisis" by Alexisonfire. *This season's growing cold, I fear that this could be the end, and there's no sign of hope, we've got a crisis on our hands. There's nothing that you can do. The sky is gonna crush you.*

I was wailing away on drums while Rhea kept the music scrolling on lead guitar. But the soundtrack kept changing; the image kept bending into strange hallucinations. The noise of the crowd was the white roar of the ocean. I looked out at their faces and they weren't people at all. They had tentacles and pinchers, and the beady black eyes of crustaceans. Then Ernest was on stage with us, playing something that sounded like a foghorn. The crowd surged toward us. Someone jumped on a table and started blowing a whistle. A referee's whistle. A spotlight fell on her. It was Ms. Cameron. She was dressed in a black-and-white striped referee's shirt, and she was blowing with puffed, red cheeks.

A whistle.

I lifted my head from the water.

A whistle.

I forced my legs into motion, the flippers sweeping through the water, treading to keep my body upright.

A whistle. Its shrill cry pierced the fog. I shook Ernest's shoulder. He lifted his head, his eyes haggard, his hair plastered over his forehead.

"Someone's coming." My voice came out in a hoarse croak.

"I saved her, Hayley. I saved Nyota," he muttered, then dropped his face back into the water.

"Hang in there," I told him. "We're getting out of this."

My lips were swollen and parched with salt. I swilled some spittle into the back of my throat, curled my tongue, stuck my thumb and index finger in my mouth, and blew. No sound. I blew again. Come on. My jawbone ached. My swollen lips vibrated with the pressure of forced air. Finally, I forced it out: a high, shrill whistle that cut through the fog. Ernest looked up. From somewhere in the fog, a whistle responded.

"They're coming, Hayley!" Ernest croaked. "They're coming!"

He grabbed me around the neck, pushing me down. I swallowed a mouthful of salt water, shoved him away and spluttered to the surface.

"Don't do that!"

"Sorry, I…"

"It's okay. Let's just get out of this."

I stuck my fingers in my mouth and whistled again. A whistle answered, louder, closer. Then a voice:

"Ernest! Hayley!"

"Here! We're over here!" Ernest's voice, jagged-edged.

The black hull of the *Zodiac* nudged through the fog. Ms. Cameron's face appeared, leaning over the edge. Her hand reached out and I caught it somehow. I never thought I'd be so glad to see a teacher. She yanked. I squirmed. Somehow we dragged my clumsy and half-numb limbs over the bulging side of the boat. Together, we reached down and each grabbed one of Ernest's arms. He screamed. We pulled. His skinny body tumbled in and rolled into the bottom of the dinghy, where he lay clutching his arm and moaning.

"What happened, Ernest? Are you okay?" Ms. Cameron crouched beside him.

"He got shot." My voice shook.

"Shot? My God, what were you kids doing out there? I told you to wait."

"We saved Nyota," Ernest babbled.

"Hush, Ernest. Can you sit up?" She tried to look at the wound in his arm, but there wasn't anything to see but a puckered hole in the neoprene.

"My God, you're frozen to the bone." She picked up his corpse-white hand. "You too, Hayley. Thank God you're alive."

She unfolded a silver, thermal space blanket from the dinghy's first-aid kit and made us huddle together underneath it. Ernest shook in violent spasms, hit by a double-whammy of shock and hypothermia. For me, the shivering came from inside, as though a deathly cold had gripped my vital organs. My stomach trembled. My lungs quivered.

I rolled myself into a ball to stop from shaking, tucking my frozen fingers beneath my knees. The boat wobbled. The outboard motor puttered, then roared, and Ms. Cameron turned us back toward the *Magdelaine.*

Ms. Cameron went on board first, helping Ernest into her small cabin in the bow. I stumbled after them, down the ladder into the galley. I barely had the energy to peel off the clammy wetsuit and fumble myself into Gram's Fair Isle sweater and a sleeping bag. Shaking, I huddled on the bench, thinking of Gram in her warm kitchen, making lobster rolls and scalloped potatoes and apple crisp.

Behind the closed door of the cabin, Ms. Cameron talked to Ernest in a soothing voice. I thought about getting up and making something hot. There was Cup-a-Soup in a cupboard. It would do me good, Gram would have said. But I didn't have the power to move. I wanted to sleep, but I couldn't do that, either. I just hunkered there in a kind of a trance, staring at nothing.

Later came the sound of someone moving around in the kitchen area. A wooden spoon thunked against a tin pot. Cutlery jangled in a drawer. The floor creaked beneath heavy boots. I didn't turn to look. I felt too stupefied to move.

"There's some soup."

A bowl of steaming chowder landed on the table in front of me. I looked up. Captain Gil.

"Thank you, Captain." He was the last person I would have pegged for a random act of kindness.

"You shouldn't've went out there," he said. I couldn't read the look on his face.

He filled another bowl from the pot on the stove and disappeared into Ms. Cameron's cabin.

The chowder tasted hot and salty, and spread warmth through my body. In my mind, I kept seeing one image over and over again: the image of the scuba tank, slipping off my back as I freed myself from the harness, and the glint of the bronze compass, attached to the harness strap, winking at me before it disappeared. Had I really seen that flash of bronze, or was guilt adding the detail to my memory— that last hope teasing me for a moment, then sinking into the darkness?

Stupid, stupid. We could've died out there. I wanted to blame Ernest, of course I did. The guy was a nutcase with his eco-hemp wardrobe and his mania for saving the planet. But in all honesty, I knew that I was the one who nearly got us killed. Ernest would have found the island, if I hadn't lost the compass. Thank God Ms. Cameron had shown up.

The door to the cabin opened and Captain Gil came out, crossed the galley and climbed to the pilothouse with his heavy tread. I hoped Ernest was going to be okay. I hoped I'd never see him again in my life.

I must have dozed off over my empty soup bowl, because I started awake when a tea-kettle whistled. Ms. Cameron stood at the stove. Her face looked drained and anxious, but she'd pulled her hair into a neat ponytail and changed into a dry sweater. It was amazing how a warm sweater could hold things together.

"Tea?" She held up the kettle. Steam poured from its spout. I nodded. Normally I didn't drink tea, but my insides still felt shaky. I added sugar and took a drink.

"How's Ernest?"

"He's sleeping," she said. "What did you kids think you were doing out there? I told you to wait for me."

"Ernest wouldn't wait," I said, and instantly felt like a bratty child, laying the blame someone else. It was my fault for losing the compass. I wondered if Ernest had told her about that.

"So you just went along with him?"

"I couldn't let him go alone."

Ms. Cameron nodded, as though acknowledging my good intentions. But I felt sick with the irony of my own words, making myself sound like a hero, when really, Ernest would have been better off without me.

"Did you see the fishing boat?" I asked.

She shook her head.

"I heard the motor when it took off. Poachers, I guess."

"Ernest was right," I said. "They did catch the sea turtle."

"You saw it?" she asked.

"Yeah, it was trapped in the net. Ernest cut it loose."

"And?"

"It dove down. It got away."

She took a long drink of tea and set the mug down on the table, cupping both hands around the warm porcelain.

"Hayley," she said. "I've never seen a sea turtle like this one. The markings, that orange starburst. It must be some kind of a rare species. And if Ernest saved it…That's much more than saving a kitten from a tree. Do you understand what I mean?"

"It's more valuable? Because it's rare?"

"Exactly. The implications for science. For conservation."

I nodded. *Look for the hero.* That was one of Dad's mottos. Crisis stories often had a hero: the mother who rushed into a burning home to save her child. The bystander who wrestled a mugger to the ground. The off-duty fireman who rescued a driver from a car wreck. People loved to read about heroes. Preferably modest and manly, but in this case they'd have to take what they could get. Ernest: fifty percent hero, fifty percent raving nutbar.

"I'm grateful that he saved the turtle. I can't pretend that I'm not," Ms. Cameron said. "But I can't have you kids putting yourselves in danger. I'm responsible for you."

"I'm here on assignment," I mumbled.

"I don't want to argue with you, Hayley. I'm responsible for Ernest. And I feel responsible for you, too. This may be a newspaper assignment, but it's also a school project. All right?"

I let her have the point.

"What do we do now?" I said.

"I don't know, Hayley. I'd like to come back out and try tagging it again, but we have to get Ernest some medical attention first. I've told the Captain to take us back to Tangiers. An ambulance is supposed to meet us there. I'm thinking that maybe we need a bigger team, more expertise. I'd like to talk to Dr. Wallis. Maybe I'm in over my head. Maybe this is too important for us to handle on our own."

"What if it's gone?" I said. "For good?"

Sea turtles might have brains the size of kidney beans, but they couldn't have existed for millions of years without some kind of survival instinct.

"It's possible," Ms. Cameron said. "It's more than possible."

She poured another mug of tea and drank. She looked as though she was thinking about something grim, and no matter which way she turned it around, she couldn't find the happy ending. The galley had grown dark and gloomy. Drizzle spattered slantwise against the portholes. The clock said seven p.m., but the dense fog made it seem later. The bare lightbulb hanging from the ceiling didn't make the place any more cheerful.

"This was supposed to be my PhD project," she said. "Instead, it's turning into a disaster."

"Your PhD?"

"You're not the only one who's ever dropped out of school, Hayley," she said.

She looked at me across the table, not in the way that a teacher usually looks at a student, like she knows everything and you know nothing. She looked at me as though we might understand each other as equals, might come to a meeting on some kind of a level plane of adulthood. She looked at me as though I might be able to hear her story and understand what she was thinking and feeling; what it might mean to look back on your life with regrets and see the places you'd messed up, and try to fix them. She looked at me, finally, like I was a journalist, and she wanted to tell me her story.

"What happened?" I said.

"I was a student of Dr. Wallis'. This was twenty years ago. We were researching a certain species of turtle. It was long days in the field, up to our knees in swamp water, getting eaten alive by mosquitoes, counting turtles. It was tedious. It was deadly boring, actually. After a while, I lost sight of the bigger picture, of why the research was important. All I knew was that if I had to spend another day counting turtles, I was going to go crazy. Remember, I was only twenty-two, twenty-three."

I nodded.

"Well, eventually, I quit. I went traveling with my boyfriend. We saw the world. It was fun, it was exciting. Eventually, I got pregnant and we settled down, had a family. I got a job teaching high school biology. There was never a good time to go back to university and pick up where I left off. But after a while, I missed it. The more I read and learned about the way that species are being driven to extinction, the more I kept thinking about the research that I could have been doing—research that would be really valuable, that might help some endangered species to survive.

"Then, a few weeks ago, I was out kayaking and I spotted this turtle. I got back in touch with Dr. Wallis. He's a professor emeritus now, and he still has an office at the university. He was so keen. He wanted me to go out and do the research. He said he'd be my thesis advisor, got everything rolling for me."

"Can you still get your PhD now?" I asked.

"I don't know. I think we'll have to find the turtle again. Otherwise..."

She took a sip of tea, set down her mug and looked at me.

"But Hayley, you can get your diploma. You've done enough work out here. Stick with it, write up your report, and I'll make sure you get the credit. Sometimes you shut a door and it takes a long time to find your way back to open it again. Don't miss the chance, now that the door's open, to walk through it."

She looked at me intently, and I knew she was asking me to buy into the moral of her story— to complete my education or I'd end up with regrets. But it seemed to me the moral of our expedition was something else. Maybe it was that the skinny kid you dismissed as a weirdo could end up doing something heroic. Maybe it was to trust your team, and they'd come through for you. Maybe it was as simple as: Don't lose your compass.

One thing I knew was that I'd be eternally grateful for the sight of Ms. Cameron, reaching through the fog over the side of that rubber dingy and offering me her hand.

"Thank you," I said.

The *Magdelaine* gave a sudden jerk. Outside, a man's voice shouted. I looked out the porthole, but it was too dark to see anything. Ms. Cameron and I climbed on deck.

A wooden wharf jutted out from a gravelly point. Night had fallen. The fog had thinned to a mist, and a floodlight at the base of the wharf cast a hazy illumination. The *Magdelaine* was churning water as Captain Gil maneuvered us into the mooring. On the wharf, a man in uniform shouted instructions. I went to the bow and threw him a line, and he fastened it to a metal cleat. It felt good to move around again. My limbs were warm and the blood had returned to my hands.

Captain Gil cut the motor. The smell of diesel fumes drifted over the bow. A Coast Guard vessel was tied up on the opposite side of the wharf. A light shone from inside its pilothouse and green and red signal lights marked the bow and stern. On the gravel road at the base of the wharf, an ambulance waited, its red emergency light strobing in circles, pulsing over the road, the rocky coast, the dark woods that hemmed in the clearing. Two paramedics hurried toward us, wheeling a stretcher. Ms. Cameron jumped on to the wharf and went to meet them.

I jumped down after her and headed toward the guy in uniform who'd tied up our boat. Time to start thinking like a reporter again. Time to kick my brain into gear. Maybe he knew something about the fishing boat and the man who'd shot at us. He was standing talking with another guy in uniform, and I figured they must both be Coast Guard officers, but when I got close enough to see their faces, it turned out I only was half-right.

The guy who'd tied up our boat was a Coast Guard officer, all right.

The other guy was RCMP Constable Alex Turpin.

Twelve

"So, you were on some kind of research project out here?"

Constable Turpin turned his head and spoke over his shoulder. From my seat in the back of the RCMP cruiser, I could see his profile backlit against the glow of the car's headlamps. He was driving up the gravel road toward the highway, while the guy from the Coast Guard rode shotgun. They'd offered me a lift back to Halifax while Ms. Cameron accompanied Ernest in the ambulance, after we'd given them our statements about the events surrounding Ernest's shooting.

"It's Ms. Cameron's project. I'm covering it," I said. "My editor wants to get some more science stories in the paper. Make it more intellectual."

Force his flunky daughter to finish high school.

"I didn't know you worked out here, Constable Turpin," I added.

"Joint training exercises with the Coast Guard," he said.

"I thought you might have been keeping an eye on the captain."

"Chiasson?" Turpin said. "Nah, that's just a coincidence. Strange one, though. How'd you convince him to let a reporter on to his boat?"

"Coincidence for me, too," I said. "Is he a suspect?"

"Suspect in what?" put in the Coast Guard guy.

Constable Turpin filled him in on the story about the bloody shack that belonged to Captain Gil, aka Hermenegilde Chiasson. I leaned forward, elbows on the seat-back, listening for any new facts that might have emerged while I was on my herpetofaunal hiatus from the civilized word. There wasn't much. The cops were treating it as a homicide, even though they hadn't found a body. They expected that if they ever did find one, it would be the body of Tyler Dervish, whose parents and friends hadn't seen him since before graduation night.

The tires of the cruiser crunched to a stop at the end of the gravel road. The headlights lit up a patch of asphalt and the yellow center-line of a two-lane highway. No cars. Just the dark shapes of trees edging up to the shoulder of the road. Constable Turpin signaled and turned.

"So is he a suspect, this captain of yours?" asked the Coast Guard guy.

"We're not ruling anyone out. But we've got no evidence against him," said Turpin. "Our guys searched his residence, nothing. He's got no connection to the victim that we can figure. And his girlfriend swears he was home in bed at the time of the murder."

"She would," the Coast Guard guy pointed out.

"Yeah. But we've still got nothing on him."

"Except the location."

"Yeah, the location. It's a shack in the woods. A hunting camp. He says he left it unlocked. Lots of guys do."

"Anyone could've walked in," the Coast Guard guy said.

"Probably someone who knew it was there, but still..."

"Could've been anyone," the Coast Guard guy said.

"Could've been anyone," Constable Turpin agreed.

The conversation in the front seat lapsed. I sat back in the darkness and zoned out to the sounds of the calls on the police radio: *car 42 to dispatch...static...dispatch to car forty-two... static...we have a report of a robbery at the Chebucto Grocery, six-three-three-zero Chebucto Road. C-H-E-B-U-C-T-O. No injuries reported...static...message received, responding...car twenty-nine to dispatch, we are returning to station...static... copy that, car twenty-nine...static...dispatch to car twenty-four... static...we have a 9-1-1 call for a child attacked by a dog in Point Pleasant Park...static...copy that, do you have an exact location?...*

My fingers itched for a notepad. Take down the exact location: Dad had drilled that into my head when he'd given me my first weekend job at the paper, the winter I turned sixteen. Soon it got to the point where Tenzen called me whenever he needed help on the crime beat. I'd covered near-fatal bar stabbings and written about kids dying in drunk-driving accidents. Most parents wouldn't want their teenager exposed to that kind of stuff, but Dad figured that if I saw the stupid tragedies that people got into with drugs and alcohol abuse, I'd be smart enough to avoid them. Dad could be a jerk sometimes, but at least he figured right about that.

Car twenty-four to dispatch, we are on location at Point Pleasant Park. This dog is still on the loose. Request backup from animal control services...

Dad would be all over the dog story. I wondered who he'd send to cover it? The summer intern, probably...that girl from the J-school program at King's, Shayla. She kept pitching political "think-pieces" and Dad kept sending her out to cover house fires and traffic fatals. That's daily news, honey. Get used to it.

The cruiser peeled off the highway at a downtown Halifax turnoff, and I leaned forward to give Constable Turpin directions to my place.

"We're heading out to the Midtown for a beer, want to join us?" he asked.

He didn't ask whether I was legally old enough to drink. I didn't enlighten him.

"Sure. I gotta get changed. Can I meet you there?"

"Yeah, no problem."

The car pulled up outside my place, a little house with a big verandah and a big yard, built back in the 1920s. Gram had left the porch light on, as usual. I opened the car door and dragged my duffle bag off the backseat. I realized then that I'd left Dr. Wallis' case with the transmitter and all the other turtle-tracking gear in the bin beneath my bunk aboard the *Magdelaine*. Ms. Cameron had been too preoccupied with getting Ernest to the hospital to worry about it, and I'd gotten sidetracked in the business of giving my statement to the Coast Guard. It probably didn't matter. I was supposed to meet up with Ms. Cameron the next morning so that we could go to see Dr. Wallis. Meanwhile, Captain Gil would bring the boat back to Halifax and we'd all regroup to figure out what to do next.

"See you soon, then," said Constable Turpin. I thought there was something warm in his voice, and maybe he smiled but I couldn't tell. There wasn't much light in the cruiser.

"See you soon."

I went in through the kitchen door and dumped my stuff on the apple-green linoleum floor. Gram was sitting at the table with three of her girlfriends, playing poker. Piles of change were heaped on the yellow-flowered tablecloth in front of them, alongside mismatched teacups and Gram's chipped Wedgewood sugar bowl. They'd left my dad's favorite wooden kitchen chair off to one side, its rungs worn into grooves where dad liked to prop his feet. The air smelled of fish and chips: Gram had never heard of nouveau cuisine, but she knew her way around a deep-fryer. It was all so normal, it hit me like culture shock after three days of chasing a giant sea turtle with a crew of social misfits.

"Sweetheart! How was your trip?" Gram got up from the kitchen table and I bent down to kiss her on the cheek. Her skin was wrinkly and soft and smelled of the same Avon Lily of the Valley perfume she'd worn since I was a little kid.

"It was insane," I said. "You should keep the door locked, Gram. There's criminals out there."

I shut the deadbolt.

"Tch! There's criminals in here," Gram waved at the card table. "Esmey's robbing me blind."

"Are you in, Betty?" Esmey tapped her cards on the table. Esmey was the chair of every volunteer organization in the neighborhood, and she liked to boss people around. Gram ignored her.

"Would you like a cup of tea, dear?" she asked me.

"That's okay, Gram. I'm going out. Is Dad around?"

"Tch!" said Gram dismissively.

I let the ladies get back to their game, and headed through the living room toward the staircase to the second floor. I needed a shower and some serious shaving to get rid of any dirt-loving parasites that might have taken up residence in my armpit hair. There was no fire burning in the living room fireplace, which was strange, even for June. Gram liked a fire in the evenings. She said it kept away her arthritis. I took a look in the firewood crib—empty. Dad was supposed to take care of the firewood, but it had obviously fallen to the back of his priority list, below late-breaking news and late-drinking with the copydeskers.

I couldn't get any grungier that I already was, so I dumped my bag on the floor, went out back to the shed and brought in a few loads of firewood. I didn't begrudge Gram, but it bugged me that Dad wouldn't do this stuff. You'd think with his mom being a widow, he'd have stepped up to the plate. But, no, Gram did everything around the house: cooked and cleaned, knitted and sewed, fixed leaky faucets and unclogged toilets.

When I was a little kid, Gram was the one who always made sure I ate a hot supper and helped me with my homework, while Dad was out chasing stories and whatever else grown men chase when they don't have a wife at home. I never asked Dad about that part of his life and he never brought a girlfriend home. But he was out late often enough. Let's just say, it wouldn't have surprised me.

In some ways, Dad still acted like a teenager and Gram still acted like his mother. And me? I'd covered enough crime to know that having someone who actually cares enough to make sure you're home for a hot dinner can make a difference between a kid who does okay in life and one who spends most of their teenagerhood in juvie. So if Gram needed firewood, I'd bring in the firewood. It didn't matter if it wasn't supposed to be my job.

I finished filling the wood crib, took a shower and changed into clean clothes: a black concert t-shirt, combat boots, and a mid-thigh-length kilt that I'd stabbed through with a hundred different-sized safety pins during a particularly crappy weekend in Grade Twelve. I threw on some lipstick, black eyeliner, and mascara, spiked my hair up with gel, and looked in the mirror.

For Heaven's sake, Hayley, you look like a porcupine. Gram's voice in my head. *Don't you want the boys to like you?*

I don't care if they like me, Gram. I want them to know I'm not a pushover. Porcupines aren't pushovers. No one messes with a porcupine.

I turned away from the mirror and grabbed my leather jacket from a hook on the wall, catching sight of my drumset that called to me from the corner of my room. Part of me wanted to chuck the whole idea of going out, crank up the tunes and wail away until I fell exhausted into bed. Part of me said I should call Rhea. Or check in with Tenzen. What did I want to go out with Constable Turpin for?

Why had he invited me out, anyways? Did he want to give me a scoop? Talk about the murder? Pump me for information about my trip with Captain Gil?

Had he smiled at me, back there in the police cruiser?

Esmey was raking up a pile of change from the center of the table when I came into the kitchen. Gram was breaking open her last roll of quarters. She looked at my getup.

"Where are you going to, dear?"

"Meeting a source."

"That's what your father always says when he's going drinking."

"I'll be good," I said.

Esmey shot me a skeptical look.

"I don't understand why these young girls feel compelled to put holes in their faces," she said, staring at my eyebrow stud. "It makes them look as though they've been shot in the head."

I resisted the urge to backtalk her. Gram would have been mortified. Instead I grabbed some bridge mix from the bowl on the table and glanced at Gram's hand. A two, a three, a seven, a jack and a king.

"Don't gamble away the laundry money," I said.

"You get out of here," she scolded.

I locked the kitchen door behind me when I left. I knew Gram wouldn't bother.

Thirteen

A twenty-minute walk took me to the Midtown Tavern. It felt good to be back in the city, with its houses and cars and shops and concrete sidewalks, and people who bathed and shaved regularly—most of them, anyways.

The Midtown had a reputation as the last blue-collar dive in downtown Halifax and the moment I stepped inside, I could see why.

There wasn't a brass tap or an oak beam in the place. No lighthouses, no puffins, no model sailing ships. No guitarist belting out "Farewell to Nova Scotia." Not a German tourist in sight. The decor consisted of dim lighting, wobbly Formica tables on a warped linoleum floor, beer signs advertising Propeller Bitter, and deep window-ledges crammed with dusty sports trophies and dead flies. A bunch of men my dad's age glanced up from their beers when I opened the door. They looked friendly but puzzled, like I must have wandered into the wrong establishment. *Oh, no, dear, you want the Liquor Dome; it's just down the way.*

"Hayley!" Constable Turpin waved to me from the back. He and the Coast Guard guy were sitting at a table covered with heaping plates of fried pepperoni and a nearly empty pitcher of beer. I went over to join them. The guys my dad's age followed me with their eyes. I was the only thing with two x-chromosomes in the place.

Constable Turpin had changed out of his uniform and into a gray t-shirt with a logo from an RCMP charity hockey tournament. It was hard not to stare at the way his t-shirt fit over his broad, athletic shoulders. The fringe of hair over his forehead was damp, like he'd just gotten out of the shower.

"Hayley, this is Constable Trevor O'Blenis," Alex said, finally giving me a proper introduction to his buddy. Constable O'Blenis had jet-black hair, a square jaw, arms that went beyond brawny into serious iron-pumping territory, and a tan that was way too deep to be natural in Nova Scotia in June. He'd changed from his uniform into a t-shirt, jeans, and Teva sandals. He looked like he belonged in one of those Hunks of the Twelfth Precinct calendars. Sexy, if you liked brute force and a badge. It was a combination I didn't trust.

Constable O'Blenis grabbed my hand and crushed it, just to show me he was the kind of guy who didn't know his own strength.

"Call me Trevor. Rhymes with 'forever,'" he said. He gave me a little twinkly look, like maybe we could get to know each other better later on. I sat down out of arm's reach.

The waiter came up and I ordered an End Wrench. That's orange juice mixed with tonic water. The name makes it sound alcoholic, but it's not, and that's why I ordered it. I don't drink a lot, especially not in a bar with two guys I don't know, but I don't like to advertise the fact that I'm not drinking, either. Weird, the way guys think that if you don't drink, you're not tough. You're not grown-up. You're just some little kid they don't have to take seriously. But really, it's the drunken girls that don't get taken seriously. That end up passed out and taken advantage of, with pictures of it plastered all over Facebook the next morning. Or pregnant with a baby they don't want. Like my mother.

That wasn't what I'd come here for. Not with Constable Turpin. Definitely not with Trevor-Forever.

I'd come here to cultivate my sources. That was it. Nothing more.

Trevor poured the last of the beer into his glass, and ordered another pitcher.

"Bring an extra glass for the lady," he said.

"No, thanks. I'm good," I said. "By the way, did you track down the guy who owns that boat? The one that shot at us?"

"The guys back at HQ checked the database. No record of a *Ferox* registered in Canada," said Trevor. "I'll request access to some foreign databases, but I probably won't get anything till at least Monday."

The waiter came back with our drinks, and I took a gulp of the orange concoction that he put in front of me. It tanged in my mouth and burned at the back of my throat going down. Whatever he'd put in the orange juice, it wasn't tonic water. Vodka? Peach Schnapps? Both? I didn't send it back, though. What was I going to do, complain it had booze in it? Trevor-Forever would get a laugh out of that.

I took another sip. *Relax, Hayley. It's just one drink.*

"So what do you do in the meantime?" I asked.

"Not much we can do. There's a thousand little coves the guy could hide in. Besides, even if we got him, the Crown might not prosecute."

"Why?"

"Slim chance of conviction. Think about it. It was a heavy fog. Could you swear a hundred percent the boat you saw was named *Ferox*? And could you swear the boat you saw was the same boat that shot at you? Maybe there were other boats around. And even if you could, what's the story here? A couple of guys go out fishing and some crazy eco-terrorist kid sneaks up and cuts their net. They take a shot at him. Yeah it's illegal, but the kid's not badly hurt. What's a jury going to think? They're going to think the kid got what was coming to him. Maybe he learned a lesson."

"But—" I stopped myself. What was I going to say? *But he saved the turtle?* I was starting to sound like an eco-freak myself. Besides, Trevor-Forever had a point. We'd been telling ourselves—Ernest, Ms. Cameron, and I—that Ernest had saved the turtle. But maybe the fishermen would've let it go anyways. After all, what could they possibly want with half a ton of herpetofauna? And besides, who was the public going to sympathize with? Ten to one, our letters to the editor would have weighed in favor of the fisherman.

"The kid who got shot, was he your boyfriend or something?" Trevor asked.

"No."

"Then forget about it. Move on."

I took another swallow of my drink and tried to think of an argument, but the Schnapps—or whatever else was in there—was already taking my edge off, making me feel warm and fuzzy. How long had it been since I'd eaten anything? I stared at the plate of fried pepperoni. The stuff was eighty percent grease, ten percent salt, and ten percent Unidentified Animal Products. Ernest would have staged an instant boycott. In this case, my stomach agreed with him.

I took another sip. How long did it take alcohol to get absorbed into the blood stream? Ms. Cameron would probably know the answer to that one. Based on my current scientific observations, I hypothesized it was close to instantaneous.

Take it easy, Hayley.

Trevor finished his beer and poured another round. Somehow a third glass had appeared on the table and he poured a beer for me, too, and I found myself drinking it. Then he ordered another pitcher. I hoped these guys weren't planning on driving.

"And another one of those orange things for the lady," said Trevor.

Not a good idea, my brain said. But my brain was becoming disconnected from my actions. Observing the events from a distance as though it might choose to intervene for my own good—or not.

The waiter brought me another drink. The guys started talking hockey

"You see the Islanders drafted Cadieux, eh?" Trevor said.

"Yeah," said Alex. "You see that play he made against Russia in the Juniors?"

"Yeah, and they say Cadieux can't skate. That's bull."

"He's leading the OHL in scoring," I put in, a little factoid I'd picked up from the sports reporter.

Trevor whistled.

"A chick who talks hockey. That's hot."

"Lay off it, Trev," said Constable Turpin.

"What? It's a compliment, Alex. She knows it's a compliment, right?"

Trevor leaned toward me, grinning.

I felt myself smiling back at him. I heard myself saying: "Right," even though I wasn't at all sure how the word had come out of my mouth. The alcohol had apparently cut off my rational mind from the instinctual part of my brain, which was now carrying on a primitive flirtation ritual with Trevor.

A waiter brought a fresh pitcher and a round of shooters: something that tasted like licorice and burned going down my throat. The guys switched to talking about football, and whether Halifax would ever get a CFL team.

"What do you think, Hayley?" Constable Alex Turpin asked.

"Great idea," I said. "You know how hard it is to fill up the Sports section when the hockey season's over?"

Trevor threw his head back and laughed.

"She's funny, too. I like this girl, Alex. How come you haven't snapped her up?"

Trevor leaned toward me. His hand, warm and heavy, landed on my thigh. I felt a throb go through my body—a throb I didn't want to feel, not for Trevor. A burning sensation flushed from my legs through my pelvis, my breasts, my neck, my lips. I caught the eyes of Constable Alex Turpin. There was something in his face: Surprise? Disappointment?

Go! shouted my rational mind. *Go! Leave! Now!*

My body didn't want to leave. My body wanted to throw itself at Trevor-Forever.

I forced myself up from my chair. The blood rushed to my head and I stumbled backwards, dizzy with hunger and alcohol. My stomach churned with a mix of bile and booze. Far across the room, I could see the red "exit" sign above the door, but it seemed impossible to make my way there. Impossible to navigate through the tables full of middle-aged beer-drinking men. I had the nightmarish feeling of being unable to move. Trevor's muscular arm wrapped itself around my waist.

"Why don't I take you home?" His voice murmured hot in my ear.

"I have to leave now." My tongue stumbled over the words. My voice sounded far away. My skin burned where Trevor touched it, between the hem of my t-shirt and the waistband of my kilt—its hundred safety-pins giving me no safety at all.

The waiter appeared at our table with a bill. Alex pulled out his wallet to pay. Trevor began steering me away, weaving me through the tables and out the door, into the hot confusion of the street.

The sidewalk was jammed with partying teenagers. Cars jostled and honked in the roadway. Headlights, lamplights, neon bar signs, lit up the scene in a crazy scramble. I took a deep breath and tried to get myself back in control.

"Let's get a cab," Trevor kissed my earlobe, my neck. I felt my body sink against his. *Relax, surrender,* said the alcohol.

Trevor pulled me tight against him. He pressed his lips down on mine. *I need to get out of here.*

I broke away and reeled backwards, bumping into strangers on the crowded sidewalk. Someone laughed. Someone asked me if I was okay. Someone steadied my elbow. I didn't want to be touched.

"Come on, sweetheart!" I heard Trevor say.

I pushed through the crowd to a taxi at the curb.

"Hayley!" I heard Alex's voice but I didn't stop, just threw myself into the cab and slammed the door behind me. I felt like an idiot, a cheap drunk, a crazy, freaked-out bitch. I sunk into the vinyl seat that smelled of beer and puke, shaking and sobbing.

"Where to, dear?" said the cabbie.

I stuttered out the address, but all I wanted to say was: "Home, take me home."

Fourteen

I woke the next morning with my alarm clock buzzing in my ears, and the icky memory of Trevor-Forever's lips on mine. A dream I couldn't recall lurked in the darkness below my conscious mind, like a troll under a bridge in a Grimm's fairy tale. A creepy feeling told me it had something to do with Trevor. *Tell me I didn't get naked with him—not even in a dream.* Why did I have to go and make an ass of myself last night?

What did Alex Turpin think of me now? That I was a cheap drunk? What did I care what he thought? I needed to focus on reporting, not getting myself mixed up with guys.

I brushed my teeth, took a shower, and brushed my teeth again. My brain felt like a bathroom drainpipe, clogged with slimy gunk. I slapped on some black eyeliner and mascara to complement the black circles under my eyes. I looked like death warmed over, but what the hell? At least I had a color scheme going.

Back in my room, I pumped up the Bad Religion tunes and dragged my body into a pair of jeans. Eight thirty. I was supposed to meet Ms. Cameron at Tim Horton's at nine. The smell of coffee, bacon, and eggs drifted up from the kitchen, along with the clatter of cutlery and the voices of Gram and

Dad. My stomach growled for breakfast, but I didn't want to hang out with Dad—a.k.a. the editor in chief. He'd be bugging me to file a story. *What've you got, Hayley? We'll take it for tomorrow. And we'll need a web-hit. What about pics?* I wasn't ready. I needed to talk to Dr. Wallis. I needed to find out how rare this turtle was, what it was, and where it came from. I needed more information about the *Ferox*, and the guys aboard it who shot at us. Most of all, I needed Dad not to see me in the shape I was in.

I stuffed my notepad, tape recorder, and camera in my bag, then caught a bus down to the harbor to pick up my car. By the time I'd made it to Tim Horton's, I was ten minutes late for our rendezvous. Ms. Cameron didn't mind; she seemed happy that I'd shown up all in one piece. No matter how bad I looked, it couldn't have been worse than when she'd hauled from the sea like a drowned rat, rescuing me from a mission gone wrong. I dumped my stuff at the molded plastic seat-and-table combo, then got in line and waited for my turn at the counter.

"Can I help who's next?"

The girl at the cash had a pale, scabby complexion, tinged violet by the fluorescent lights of the overhead menu board. I stepped up to the counter and nearly gagged on the smell of burnt coffee and drive-thru gasoline fumes. On the menu board, an illuminated picture of chunky chicken noodle soup beamed at me, larger than life. Ugh.

"Diet Coke, chocolate-dip donut, and a bottle of orange juice." At least the orange juice had vitamins in it.

I put my tray down opposite Ms. Cameron. She still had the Eddie Bauer look going: a long khaki skirt, cotton blouse, and Birkenstock sandals.

"How's Ernest doing?" I asked.

"He's all right. We'll pick him up on our way to Dr. Wallis' office. How are you?"

"I'm okay."

"Good. I wanted to talk to you."

I bit into the chocolate-dip donut.

"Should I get out my notepad?"

"No. I...Actually, that's what I wanted to talk to you about."

I took another bite and waited. My head pounded with a bass-heavy backbeat.

"I want you to be discreet, Hayley, when we go to talk to Dr. Wallis this morning. He's a very eminent scientist. We should be grateful that he's taking the time to meet with us, especially on a Saturday morning."

Getting up early on a weekend to discuss reptiles—how could you not be grateful for that? Still, I wasn't sure what she was driving at.

"How do you mean, discreet?"

"I told Dr. Wallis that you were a student of mine. I didn't tell him you were a newspaper reporter. I think it would be better if we could just leave it at that."

"You mean not tell him that I'm writing a story?"

Ms. Cameron nodded.

"I have to tell him I'm writing a story, if I'm going to quote him," I said.

"Quote him? Oh, no, you can't quote him." Ms. Cameron looked appalled.

"Why not? That's my job."

"Yes, I understand that, Hayley. But not in this case."

"Why not?"

"Because—well, because Dr. Wallis doesn't really like the media."

Somehow, I should've seen that coming.

"No one likes the media, but everyone reads the news. Why is that?"

"This is a bit of a special case, Hayley. He had a very bad experience with a reporter once."

"So that means...what? He'll never speak to another reporter again?" I said. "What if he had a bad experience with a checkout clerk? Would he stop buying groceries?"

"Just listen, Hayley, and let me explain."

Ms. Cameron paused and took a sip of coffee. I looked at my unopened cans of orange juice and Diet Coke. Sugar or caffeine? I opted for caffeine.

"You see," she began, "when I was studying under Dr. Wallis twenty years ago, he was the most prominent scientist in Canada in his field—the evolutionary biology of reptiles. He was being considered for a promotion to Dean of Science. It was an intense competition, but we all thought he would get it. All his students, I mean. He was a fantastic teacher and a brilliant researcher. And it was the right time in his life. He was in his late fifties, a seasoned teacher. He'd already climbed the ladder, contributed a lot to the university, raised its scientific profile. Then, just before the meeting when the Board of Directors was supposed to choose the successful candidate, a newspaper story came out.

"There was a front page photo: Dr. Wallis, posing with a gun beside the carcass of a dead polar bear. Somehow, the journalist had found out that he'd spent the summer on a big game hunting expedition in the Arctic. I don't know where she got the photo; one of his hunting companions, I suppose. It was all perfectly legal. He had the proper license and an Inuit guide. But what a controversy! The environmental groups were up in arms. People wrote letters to the University chancellor. What was a prominent biologist doing, killing polar bears for sport? That wasn't the image the university wanted to project.

"The Board of Directors caved to public pressure. They appointed some obscure chemistry professor to the position. Dr. Wallis retired a few years later. They appointed him professor emeritus and let him keep his office on campus, but it didn't change the fact that the newspaper story essentially ruined his career. So you see, Hayley, I can't show up on his doorstep with a reporter."

I nodded like I was full of sympathy for the poor guy. But what I really wanted to say was: Great story. Heck of a reporting job. And if the guy had really wanted to be dean of science, maybe he shouldn't have been up there killing polar bears in the first place.

"That was twenty years ago, though, right?" I said. "I bet he's got over it by now."

"I don't know, Hayley. I only recently got back in touch with him. Just for this project, really."

So that was it. She didn't want to screw up her chances at getting her PhD by aggravating Dr. Wallis.

"Look, Hayley. Just come along to the meeting," Ms. Cameron pleaded. "Listen to what he has to say, learn from it, and work it into your article. Just don't mention his name. You can do that, can't you?"

I thought about it as I downed the last of my Diet Coke. It ticked me off to agree to that kind of deal, just to keep my teacher happy. Dad didn't like printing stories with unnamed sources. He said it undermined the credibility of the paper. And then, what if he said something totally quote-worthy, and I couldn't quote him? That was the problem with letting people go off the record.

But still, I couldn't shake the image of Ms. Cameron, coming through the fog in that rubber dingy, hauling me over the side of the boat. I owed her a lot. Like my life.

Certainly, I owed her enough not to screw up her chances at a PhD.

"Okay," I said. "Fine."

"Thank you, Hayley," said Ms. Cameron. "Let's go get Ernest."

Fifteen

The lawn in front of Ernest's house looked too grassy-green to be organic. His dad probably came out early on Sunday mornings to spray it with pesticides while Ernest lay in bed, deciding what kind of granola to eat for breakfast. Given the way his wife had left him for a life of probiotic lesbian farming, he probably felt sweet revenge every time he blasted a dandelion.

Ernest had showered and shaved since I'd last seen him, which marginally improved his appearance. His arm was in a sling, and he smelled of patchouli—a sharp odor, like sandalwood mixed with BC bud, that made me think of campgrounds full of guys in goatees and knitted berets. He looked as wrung-out as an over-bleached dishrag. Gram would have sat him down at the kitchen table and stuffed him full of roast beef and mashed potatoes, but he was probably trying to rebuild his iron supplies with sautéed kale and spinach smoothies. Good luck with that.

"How's it going?" I said. I could barely look him in the eye, still feeling guilty over the way I'd lost the compass.

Ernest shrugged his one good shoulder.

"I'm okay."

He rode to the university in Ms. Cameron's car while I followed in the Firefly, which was a relief, since I didn't have to make conversation with him. We wound along curved driveways past the grassy lawns of the campus and pulled up in the parking lot in back of the gray stone Biology building.

Our footsteps rang in the empty hallways as we made our way to Dr. Wallis' office on the second floor. Ms. Cameron tapped on the heavy oak door and it swung open to reveal Dr. Wallis looming before us, more gaunt and towering that I'd remembered him. He wore a tweed suit and a moss-green dress shirt, and he held in his right hand a dark wooden cane with a silver tip and an ivory handle, carved in an intertwining motif of animals, jungle vines, and tiny grimacing human faces.

"My dear Nora! It's a pleasure to see you!" he wheezed. "And your young students. Please come in."

The small, square room fit the bill for a professor's office. Two walls were covered with floor-to-ceiling shelves, every shelf stuffed with books and papers. A huge wooden desk stood against the third wall, beneath a window that overlooked a grassy quad and a scattering of gray-stone university buildings. Glossy posters of reptiles hung on the final wall. A large leather swivel-chair sat beside the desk; two small wooden chairs were crammed tightly into a corner.

Covering nearly the entire floor-space was a huge, polar-bear skin rug, its teeth bared in a perpetual snarl at anyone coming through the door. Apparently, Dr. Wallis' last laugh against the Board of Directors.

Ms. Cameron and I stepped inside. Ernest stopped in the doorway.

"That's a polar bear," he said.

"It's perfectly dead, I assure you." A glint came into Dr. Wallis' sunken eyes. "I shot it myself."

"Polar bears are an endangered species." Ernest's voice quavered.

"So they tell you," Dr. Wallis waved a hand. "The self-styled environmentalists who've never been farther north than the end of the Toronto subway line. Well, I have been to the Far North and let me assure you that the Arctic contains a healthy breeding population of *Ursus maritimus*. Now come in, and let's get down to the business of our sea turtle."

Dr. Wallis turned his back on Ernest and lowered himself creakily into the swivel chair. Ernest stood swaying in the doorway. He looked so weak, you could've knocked him over with a well-aimed tennis ball, but you had to admire the way he didn't let a little blood loss get in the way of his fanaticism.

"Ernest," Ms. Cameron said. "Please come in."

He shook his head.

"I won't. I can't."

Dr. Wallis swiveled toward him.

"Young man," he wheezed, "do you know that I paid an Inuit guide ten thousand dollars for the privilege of shooting that polar bear? I have the legal hunting license framed on the wall." He jabbed a finger at it. "Ten thousand dollars. Do you know what that means in terms of food? And clothing? And fuel? Tell me, what industries are there in Nunavut, apart from soapstone carving and government handouts? How else is an Inuit man with less than a high school education to earn a living? Or do you wish for the Inuit to go back to living in igloos, killing caribou with stone weapons, and starving in the winter if the hunt fails? That's very progressive of you. Off you go, then, set up your tent in the woods and gather your roots and berries. Or stop this fooling around and let's get down to business."

Dr. Wallis drew a deep, rasping breath. The air seemed to catch in his throat and he gaped, open-mouthed as though his breathing reflex had failed. An ashen tinge crept across his lips and the skin of his face. He hunched forward, leaning all his weight on his cane. His chest spasmed and a fit of hoarse, choking coughs wracked his body. Ms. Cameron grabbed a glass of water from his desk and tried to fit it into his hand, but he waved it away, fumbled instead for a pocket handkerchief to wipe up the blood-specked phlegm. At last the coughing fit passed and he leaned on his cane, gasping, reaching for the water glass that Ms. Cameron held out to him.

She shot a look at Ernest and he slunk into the room, skirting the bearskin rug, and slid into one of the wooden chairs. I took the seat beside him.

"Please excuse me, Nora," said Dr. Wallis at last. "Now, tell me about your sea turtle."

Ms. Cameron gave him the rundown, while I got out my camera and hooked it up to Dr. Wallis' computer. The pictures flashed on to the screen. Some showed the turtle from above, the orange starburst splayed across its mottled shell. Others showed it from the front, its leathery face staring into the camera with the inscrutable expression of an ancient hermit.

"Extraordinary," Dr. Wallis muttered, scrolling through the photos. "I knew you'd found something special. But this—this is truly...extraordinary..."

"I was hoping you could help me to identify the species," said Ms. Cameron, looking over his shoulder at the screen. "I couldn't tell..."

"Yes, yes, of course you couldn't tell, Nora. The species? Ah, the species!" Dr. Wallis swiveled around, making Ms. Cameron step backwards against an overstuffed bookshelf. Pressing heavily on the armrests, he drew himself to his feet and took a step toward the wall of reptile posters. He seemed suddenly full of energy, almost feverish.

"The species, yes! That's precisely the thing, isn't it? The species!" He coughed, unable to speak for a minute, but finally cleared his throat and tapped his cane on a poster that showed a montage of sea turtles against a watery background.

"There are seven known species of sea turtle alive today. The Loggerhead. The Kemp's Ridley. The Olive Ridley. The Hawkesbill. The Flatback. The Green Turtle. And the Leatherback. Which one does yours look like?"

"But it doesn't look like any of them," she shook her head. "Not any."

"Precisely!" Dr. Wallis tapped his cane again. "That's precisely it, Nora! It doesn't...look...like...any...of...them."

"I don't understand."

"Just let me sit down. And I shall give you an introductory lecture into the evolutionary biology of sea turtles."

As Dr. Wallis eased himself back into the swivel chair, I got out my notepad. Dad wanted science, Dad was going to get science. Serve him right for trying to elevate the tone of the paper.

"It begins two hundred and forty million years ago, in the Triassic era, the time of the early dinosaurs," Dr. Wallis began. "The ancestor of the turtles was a mid-sized reptile, probably the size and shape of an iguana. It was not significantly different from any other reptile, until a single genetic mutation occurred which would change its destiny as a species."

Dr. Wallis leaned forward and fixed his eyes on Ms. Cameron.

"Imagine a clutch of eggs, laid in the warm sand of this prehistoric world. During the embryonic development of those eggs, a strange thing occurs. The rib-bones of these tiny embryos do not grow into a normal ribcage. Instead, they fuse together to form a bony shell. Yes, Nora, a shell, which sets these creatures apart from all other reptiles, and which remains the characteristic trait of all turtles down to the present day."

He paused and took a drink of water.

"Think about it. A shell. Protection not only from predators, but from other hazards. Chemicals. Ultra-violet radiation. Physical shocks. Through the process of evolution, these early turtles gave rise to the great land tortoises, and to the freshwater turtles, and to the mighty pelagic sea turtles that took to the oceans—we don't know exactly when—but certainly by the time of the Cretaceous era.

"You'll recall the Cretaceous era, Nora. Dinosaurs ruled the land, and fearsome reptiles terrorized the seas. The Kronosaurus, an eleven-ton carnivore that could rip apart a great white shark. The plesiosaurs that looked like swimming brontosauri, with their long necks to catch fish from the deep or snatch pterodactyls from the air. And sea turtles, many species of sea turtles.

"Then came the great meteor strike, sixty-five million years ago, that killed the dinosaurs. It killed the great marine reptiles, too. All except the sea turtles. Yes, the sea turtles survived. But not all of them. Of the many species of sea turtles that swam in the prehistoric ocean, as I said, only seven remain that we know of today."

Dr. Wallis gestured at the turtles in the poster:

"Seven." He swiveled toward the computer screen with the photo that I'd taken of our monstrous turtle. "Seven. And this one doesn't look like any of them."

"Eight," whispered Ms. Cameron.

"Eight," said Dr. Wallis.

"A new species," she said, her voice edged with excitement.

"New to science, but in fact, very old." Dr. Wallis leaned forward. "As old as the dinosaurs."

A living dinosaur. Now we were talking headlines. Dad was going to love it. And I had pictures. Exclusive pictures

"A sea turtle that everyone thought had gone extinct." Dr. Wallis reached a book down from one of the shelves and opened it to a glossy color plate. "An Archelon—the greatest of all the sea turtles. In the Cretaceous, they grew to a diameter of fifteen feet and could weigh three tons. This one is much smaller, but it bears a strong resemblance to the fossil record."

"But how could it have been here all this time and no one knew about it?" Ernest burst out.

"An excellent question," said Dr. Wallis. "The fact is, sea turtles spend most of their lives in the open ocean. They return to shore only once a year, to lay their eggs. What if a small colony of Archelon survived through all these millions of years? Not here in Nova Scotia, but on some remote, uninhabited island, a mere speck of sand in the vast ocean. Isn't it possible? It must be possible. Otherwise, these photographs could not exist."

"But why has it suddenly appeared?" asked Ms. Cameron. "Why here? Why now?"

I leaned over and whispered to Ernest: "Maybe it showed up for the Highland Games."

He shushed me with an annoyed look on his face. I thought about telling him to get a sense of humor—it might help him with the girls. But who was I to give dating advice, considering my fiasco the night before with Constable Turpin and Trevor-Forever?

"For millions of years, Nora, the ocean was a relatively stable environment," Dr. Wallis said. "But in the past century, it has changed rapidly. Ocean liners and container ships have turned parts of the sea into highways. Marine animals have fled, or faced death. Offshore drilling for oil and gas has put entire ecosystems in peril. Factory trawlers are so huge they carry entire fish processing plants on deck. Fish populations have plummeted. Global warming is changing the temperature of the waters, forcing animals out of their historic ranges. The ocean is in a state of disruption, Nora. And I am convinced that if the disruption of war creates human refugees, the disruption of ecosystems can create animal refugees. Perhaps this creature was injured and disoriented in a collision with a ship. Perhaps its food supply ran out. Perhaps the area where it lived was contaminated by an oil spill. Perhaps that's why, after living peacefully in an isolated part of the ocean for millions of years one of these turtles suddenly arrives here, in a spot inhabited by humans."

The effort of his long lecture had taken the wind out of Dr. Wallis. He leaned back in his chair, eyes half-closed, and raised the water glass to his lips.

"We have to find it again." Ms. Cameron's voice was urgent. "We have to get that GPS tracker on it."

"Such a missed opportunity!" said Dr. Wallis.

"I'm sorry. As I told you, the drill bit broke when I was trying to drill the shell..."

The drill bit? I glanced at Ernest and caught on his face a fleeting glimpse of surprise and gratitude for Ms. Cameron's lie.

"God Almighty! I wish I'd gone out there myself!" Dr. Wallis cursed.

"I'll go out again. But I'm concerned about my students."

Dr. Wallis rubbed his forehead with his large, liver-spotted hand.

"Yes. You told me about that...incident." He looked at the sling on Ernest's arm.

"It's nothing," Ernest said. "I'm fine. I can go back."

"I'm going too," I said.

"I'm not sure..." Ms. Cameron looked at Dr. Wallis.

"We must consider our next step carefully," he said. "Give me a little time, Nora, to think this over. To gather my resources. Perhaps we need a bigger boat. A larger crew. I'll be in touch soon and let you know my plans. Above all, we mustn't let it slip away. Think of the value..."

"To science," said Ms. Cameron.

"Of course, to science."

He rose and opened the door.

"You must all understand the importance of keeping quiet about this," he said. "Above all, we mustn't let anyone else know about it before we've staked our claim. If word were to get out, there would be a mad rush. Competing research teams. Gawkers. Poachers. The media."

"Of course," said Ms. Cameron.

"I'll hold you responsible, then, Nora," said Dr. Wallis. He saw us out and closed the door behind us.

"A new species!" Ernest's voice rang in the empty hall. "A dinosaur turtle! This is fantastic!"

"The guy just told us to keep our mouths shut about it," I reminded him.

"I hope I won't be reading about it in the paper tomorrow, Hayley." Ms. Cameron put her hand on my shoulder.

"I'll hold the story," I said. Dr. Wallis was right that the media hordes would descend as soon as word got out. It wouldn't do me any good to have competitors elbowing me out of the way, scaring off the turtle before we could get a GPS transmitter on it. As long as it remained our secret, I could break the story in my own time.

"But I want to come along when you go out there again," I added.

"Hayley, I'm not sure it's safe..."

"I'll take my chances," I said. "But if you leave without me, I've got to tell my editor about it. And once he knows, he'll put it in the paper before anyone else scoops us. Believe me, a living dinosaur is front page news."

Sixteen

The turtle story had stalled just when it was starting to get interesting and I felt as restless as a hunting dog with nothing to hunt. I thought about calling Alex to find out if Trevor-Forever had discovered the owner of the *Ferox*, but I didn't know what I'd say to him—*Hi, Alex, this is Hayley. That crazy girl who ran out on you guys last night?*—so I decided to call Tenzen instead and catch up on the cop beat.

Tenzen didn't answer his cell. I left a message and spent a few minutes thinking my way back into the story of the bloody shed and the disappearing drug dealer. That was when I remembered that Rhea might have heard something about Tyler Dervish through her network of stoner friends.

I rang the bell at Rhea's house and her mother told me to go up to her room. Rhea's mom thought I was a good influence, which said a lot about the other kids that Rhea hung out with.

The light in her bedroom was off, the window-shade pulled down. The only signs of Rhea were a lumpy shape under the blanket and a tangle of black hair splayed over the white pillowcase. I opened the window-shade and sat down on the bed beside the lump.

"Rhea."

She turned her head and squinted at me.

"Oh God, it's early." Her voice crackled in the back of her throat.

"It's almost noon."

"Oh God."

She closed her eyes.

"Rhea, I gotta talk to you about Tyler. Tyler Dervish."

"Tyler Dervish," she mumbled. "I don't know anything about him."

"The cops think he's dead."

"I think *I'm* dead."

"Rhea." I shook her. "What have you heard? Anything? What are people saying?"

Rhea groaned, rolled over on her back and brushed the hair out of her face. The skin on her cheeks was marked with red lines from the folds in the pillowcase. Her hair reeked of cigarette smoke.

"Oh, God, Hayley. Get me a drink of water."

I found a mug in the bathroom, filled it and came back. Rhea drained it in one gulp.

"I need a joint," she said.

"You need to get off that shit."

She pressed the cold mug against her forehead.

"Did I tell you? I got accepted into Pharmacology at McGill. Ironic, eh? I figure I'll quit after I find out what it's doing to my brain."

"It's frying your brain. I could tell you that, and save you a couple thousand bucks in tuition."

"Get off my case, Hayley."

"Okay, fine. Tyler. Tyler Dervish."

She ran her hand through the knots in her hair. On the underside of her upraised arm, a red prick-mark showed on white skin.

"I thought you didn't do the hard stuff."

She jerked her arm down.

"I gave blood. Okay?"

"Rhea—"

"Hayley—"

"Okay, fine. Just tell me about Tyler."

"All's I know is, he was supposed to meet this guy, Snake."

"This was when?"

"Before, you know…"

"Before Chuck and Phil found that shack?"

"Yeah."

"Snake?"

"Yeah. And he was scared shitless."

"Why?"

"Because he owed him money. That's why he was supposed to meet him, to pay him back. Only he didn't have it. That's how come I knew about it. Because Tyler wanted to borrow money from me to pay back Snake."

"Did you give it to him?"

"No. Do you think I'm stupid?"

"Okay. This guy Snake, what's his real name?"

Rhea shrugged.

"I dunno. He's older. Like, in his thirties or something."

"You know what he looks like?"

"I've seen him around."

"You know where I can find him?"

Rhea turned her head and stared out the window.

"Rhea, where can I find him?"

"You're not going to talk to him, are you Hayley? You're crazy, you know."

"I didn't say I was going to talk to him. I just want to know how to find him."

"I don't know his address or anything."

"But you know where to find him."

"All's I know is where he was partying last night."

"Jesus, Rhea! You were partying with him?"

She turned to look at me again. The skin on her face was as white and fine as porcelain. Rhea had this china-doll beauty that she was doing her best to ruin with smoking and partying. Her hair fell over her face and she pulled it back, kept one hand gripped tight in the tangle of black curls.

"Well I didn't know he was going to be at the party when I went there, did I Hayley?"

"You could've left."

"My boyfriend was there. A lot of people."

"Where did Snake go after the party?"

"That's what I'm trying to tell you, Hayley. Everyone was planning on crashing overnight."

"You didn't."

"Yeah. Because I've got this stupid thing called a two a.m. curfew. My mom would've tracked me down. Trust me. She's got a GPS-chip installed on my cell phone."

"But Snake? He was crashing at the party?"

"Yes. That's what I'm trying to tell you."

"Okay. What's the address?"

"I dunno Hayley. It was one of those...you know. One of those places." She waved her hand vaguely and let it fall to the blanket.

"You know how to get there?"

She nodded.

"Okay. Let's go."

I pulled a pair of jeans and a t-shirt out of her dresser and threw them on the bed.

"What?"

"Let's go. You can show me where the place is. You can point out the guy to me. Snake."

"Are you crazy, Hayley? You can't just go up and talk to him. For all you know, he could've killed Tyler. Besides, even if he crashed there, he's probably already gone by now."

"I didn't say I was going to talk to him. I just want to see what he looks like. Get his real name." *Get a photo.*

"How are you going to get his real name?"

"He's got a car, right?"

"A truck."

"Right. So I take down the license plate number, get his name from Motor Vehicle Registration."

"You can do that?"

"Yeah."

"How do you know this stuff?"

"I'm a reporter, Rhea," I said. "Come on. Let's go."

I followed Rhea's directions to Lawrencetown, a shabby neighborhood where the city peters out into scrubby countryside, not farmland and not a suburb, just a string of overgrown lots forgotten by developers. She pointed me down a pot-holed, two-lane road dotted with trailer homes and broken-down bungalows. The houses were set far back from the road, as though they didn't trust each other, didn't want to get too close. The front lawns sprouted weeds and rusted-out vehicles.

"There it is," Rhea said finally, pointing to a one-story rectangle covered in dented blue aluminum siding. A bunch of cars and trucks were parked haphazardly in front of it, some in the gravel driveway, some in the scrubby front yard. A chained pit bull lay on the front step with its head on its paws, watching the road.

"Jesus, Rhea," I said. "You came here to party?"

"You sound like my mom, Hayley. It's a bunch of musicians that live here, okay? They're good guys."

"It looks like a crack house," I said.

A row of scrubby hedges marked the border of the property. On the lot just beyond it, a gravel driveway, overgrown with weeds, led to an abandoned a tarpaper shack with the roof half caved-in. I pulled into the shack's driveway behind the screen of hedges and stopped the car amid the weeds. Camouflaged as a derelict vehicle, the Firefly fit right in.

"What are we going to do now?" said Rhea.

"Wait for him to come out."

We rolled down all the windows, but it still got hot inside the car as the sun blazed in the early afternoon sky. Insects buzzed in the weeds and wildflowers. From somewhere came the putter-and-roar of a chainsaw. I was dozing off when a screen door banged and the demented barking of a dog cut through the lazy summer air.

"That's him," hissed Rhea. "That's Snake."

I could see him fairly clearly through the screen of the hedges, standing on the concrete stoop in front of the house. Snake had burly shoulders and a beer gut, dark brown beard, baseball cap shoved down over dark brown hair. He was texting something on a cell phone when the dog jumped up on him, trying to lick his face. Snake shoved it back. The dog skidded with a yelp across the front stoop and fell halfway down the stairs, scrambled onto its legs and squirmed toward Snake, fawning and crouching. Snake unhooked it from its chain and shouted a command. The dog ran and jumped into the back of a dirty red pickup truck. Snake followed, clipped the dog's collar to a chain in the back of the truck, and got into the truck's cab.

I ducked down low in my car as the truck drove past. I let it go a bit down the road, then put my car in gear and followed.

"What are you doing, Hayley?" said Rhea. She slouched low in her seat and mussed her hair over her face, afraid of being seen.

"I need to get the license plate number."

I came up as close behind the truck as I dared, but the tires kicked up dust on the gravel road and the plate was caked with mud, too dirty to make out the numbers.

"Let's go home," said Rhea.

I ignored her and followed Snake.

The road ended in a T-junction. Snake's truck took a right-hand turn onto Highway 107, leading away from Halifax. I waited until there were a couple of cars between us on the highway, then turned to follow it.

"What are you doing?" said Rhea.

"I bet he's going home. If I get his address, I might be able to find out his real name through the land registry."

"Who cares about his real name?" said Rhea.

"I do."

Rhea turned away, her long black hair blowing wildly in the wind that whipped through the open window. The car directly in front of me was a monster Buick with license plates that said "Idaho—Famous Potatoes!" Seemed like Idaho was scraping the bottom of the fame barrel.

We drove eastward for about twenty minutes, then Snake took a turnoff marked "scenic route," followed by the Idaho Famous Potatoes car. I turned behind them. The road meandered along the coastline, winding among bays and woodlands. It was one of those roads that tourists drive in the hopes of finding spectacular ocean views and quaint souvenir shops. The Idahoans were definitely in the right place, but what was

Snake doing here? Cruising the kitsch shops for a lobster-shaped beer-bottle opener? Somehow I doubted it.

The Famous Potatoes people slowed down to enjoy the view, and as the road dipped and curved, I caught glimpses of Snake's red truck getting further and further ahead. We crested a hill where a scenic ocean vista opened up before us and I slammed on the brakes just in time to avoid rear-ending the Idahoans, who'd slowed down even more to take in the view. Below, Snake's red pickup disappeared around a bend.

All the way down the hill, I rode the brake and ground my teeth. Finally I couldn't take it anymore, stepped on the gas and started to pull across the solid yellow line, when a logging truck came barreling around the bend in the opposite direction. I swerved back into my lane and hit the brakes. The Famous Potatoes car dawdled ahead.

We'd lost sight of the ocean now, and the road dipped and curved through woodlands. The miles and minutes passed. I didn't catch another sight of Snake's truck. Rhea sat silently in the passenger seat, her head leaning against the window. I couldn't tell if she was sleeping, or just mad at me and not talking. Every time I thought about pulling out to pass, another eighteen-wheeler would come roaring around a blind curve and make me change my mind. I turned on the radio—some lame best-hits-of-the-seventies-eighties-and-nineties station. I was about to give up and find a place to pull a U-turn, when suddenly I spotted Snake.

The red pickup had pulled off the highway, onto a dirt lane that cut into the woods. It was parked in front of a high, wrought-iron gate between two massive, stone pillars. Snake was just getting out of the cab.

I drove past the truck and continued over a hill. At the bottom of the hill, a clearing in the woods marked a rest-stop on the side of the highway. There wasn't much to it: a concrete washroom plunked decoratively in the middle of a gravel parking lot, with a few lopsided wooden picnic tables scattered around. I parked my car behind the washroom building, out of sight of the road.

"Huh?" said Rhea. She wiped her eyes and blinked at me.

"I'm going to have a look around," I said.

"Where are we?"

"I'm not sure. Maybe Snake's place. Want to come?"

"You're crazy, Hayley. I'm staying in the car."

"Okay. Don't open the door to strangers."

"Duh."

I jammed a notepad and pen into one back pocket, my cell phone into the other, slung my camera over my shoulder and set out through the woods.

Seventeen

The hill that led to the iron gate seemed a lot steeper on foot than it had when I'd cruised down it in the Firefly. I dug my sneakers into the dirt, swatting mosquitoes and dodging cedar branches. Just when I thought my wilderness adventures were over, here I was chasing a drug dealer through Canada's boreal backwaters. At least Ernest hadn't tagged along.

I reached the top of the hill and dropped to my knees in the underbrush. Below, the dirt road stood empty. Snake's truck had disappeared. The gate was closed, a metal cross-bar holding it shut.

I worked my way down the side of the hill, grabbing branches as my boots skidded through the loose dirt and set off tiny avalanches of rocks and twigs. I looked around for a mailbox or something that might give me the address of the place, but there was nothing. Just the gate, the stone pillars, and a chain-link fence anchored to the pillars that cut through the forest, marking the perimeter of the property.

The gate wasn't locked. It wouldn't be hard to open the cross-bar and waltz straight up the driveway. But that seemed like tempting fate, and since I'd already rejected Death by Speeding Logging Truck that day, I figured I'd rather avoid

Death on a Country Estate, as well. Instead, I grabbed hold of the nearest stone pillar and rock-climbed up until I was hanging on to the big, carved-stone sphere at the top. The mosquitoes whined in my ears. I edged my way around to the other side of the pillar. My chin scraped against the rough stone, leaving a bloody smear. DNA evidence, in case anyone ever had to investigate my mysterious disappearance. I let go of the pillar and dropped to the ground inside the fence.

A thick undergrowth of tangled vines and prickly brambles crunched beneath my combat boots. I swatted the air around my head, trying to fend off the swarm of mosquitoes. After about fifty steps, the woods ended at the edge of a wide, landscaped lawn that swept up to a huge stone mansion. If this was Snake's house, he must have been making a killing off the drug trade. But if that was the case, what was he doing partying in a rundown bungalow in Lawrencetown?

Maybe it belonged to his boss, or a client. Maybe Tyler wasn't dead and Snake was keeping him here, a hostage until he got paid the money Tyler owed him. Finding Tyler Dervish alive—that would be a great scoop.

The pickup truck was parked at the top of a curving driveway. I zoomed in with my camera, trying to make out an address on the front entrance of the house, but if there was one, I couldn't see it. Couldn't get a fix on the truck's plates, either. In the back of the truck, the pit bull stood alert.

I took a few steps back into the woods and I followed the cover of trees around to the back of the mansion. Here, the forest closed in nearer to the house, and I crept to within spitting distance of a mossy stone patio that led inside via a pair of French doors. No human voices, only the whine of mosquitoes and the incongruously cheerful chirping of birds. The French doors were closed, the view inside blocked by heavy curtains, but through a gap in the curtains I could see a sliver of what looked like a formal library or study. I zoomed in. On the back wall, a dark wooden mantelpiece, carved with elaborate curlicues, framed a large fireplace. In front of the fireplace stood a wooden desk, carved in the same style. Propped against the desk was a hunting rifle.

Snake crossed my field of vision, then crossed again, pacing the room. He seemed to be talking to someone, but whoever it was stayed out of sight.

I lowered my camera and surveyed the stone patio. At the far side, an ornamental gate led into a rose garden surrounded by a rustic stone wall. Through the iron bars of the gate, I could see a large pond in the middle of the garden with a marble fountain rising from its center. It was one of those fake-Italian things, with three tiers of fluted basins topped by a statue of a nymph or goddess carrying a water-jug. Presumably, the water was supposed to pour from her jug down the tiers of the fountain, but the whole thing was overgrown with moss and looked like it hadn't been operational for several years.

Near the garden, three shallow steps led down from the stone patio to a footpath that wound its way into the woods, away from the house. The path was covered in glistening white crushed stone, making it easy to keep in sight while I followed it, staying under the cover of the trees.

A breeze rustled the leaves, bringing a tang of salt to the musty air of the forest. The wind picked up as I continued beside the path, until I heard the screech of seagulls and the noise of waves beating against a rocky shore. At last the woods gave way to open sky, the wind blew the mosquitoes away and I stood at the top of a cliff, overlooking a small bay.

To my right, at the end of the stone path, a zigzag staircase led down the cliff. At the bottom of the cliff, a wooden dock jutted into the water. Tethered to the dock was an expensive-looking fishing boat. White, with a sky-blue stripe on the hull.

A sky-blue stripe.

Just like the *Ferox*.

I swung my camera around and zoomed in on the boat, but couldn't make out the name. Maybe it wasn't the *Ferox*, just a boat that looked like her. What did I know about boats, anyways? And what could Snake have to do with the *Ferox*? Drug dealers and fishermen? It didn't make any sense.

Beside the dock was a concrete boat-launching ramp and a gravel road that sloped upward, disappearing into a cut in the cliff. Seagulls swooped and screamed. Waves beat against the rocks. No one was down there. No one was on the staircase. No one was on the gravel road or the white-pebbled footpath.

The Ferox. Go down there and have a look.

Stupid. Crazy.

Just do it.

I crept to the stairway, turned two zigzags and stopped on the landing halfway down the cliff-face, heart hammering. The wooden handrail felt warm beneath my palms, its rough wood damp with spray. I gripped it and leaned over to look below. The dock was still deserted. The waves beat against the shore. The salt air was heavy with the smell of seaweed. All I needed was to zoom in close enough to make out the name on the stern of the boat. It made me feel dizzy, though, leaning over that wooden handrail. Nothing to hold me if the old wood gave out. I lay down instead, my stomach and thighs pressing against the wood planks. I could feel the gaps between them; see through the gaps to the stomach-churning waters below. I propped up my elbows, held the camera steady and zoomed in on the black patch of lettering against the white hull.

Ferox.

Hot damn.

I shot a few frames then zoomed out and shot the entire boat. Evidence. But evidence of what? What could Snake possibly have to do with the *Ferox*? It would help if I knew where the hell I was. If I had an address, or a GPS function on my phone...

Truck tires crackled on gravel but my mind barely registered the sound. I shot a few more frames. Then the bark of a dog echoed off the cliff and I tore my eye away from the camera, to the sight of Snake's truck parked on the concrete boat ramp beside the dock. In the back of the truck, his dog barked, a mindless, repeated quarter-note: Arp! Arp! Arp! Arp! Arp! Arp! Arp! Arp!

Snake got out of the cab and walked toward the boat.

An electronic jangle cut through the air. Shit. I grabbed my cell phone from my back pocket. Below, Snake stopped in his tracks. I jammed a thumb on a button to turn the phone off, but hit the 'talk' button by mistake.

"Hayley?" came a voice.

Alex Turpin. Oh, Christ. This was not the time to say whatever needed to be said about last night.

I hit the power-off button. The phone jingled its little electronic good-bye song. This time Snake's head jerked up. He shielded his eyes with his hand, scanning the top of the cliff. I pressed myself against the deck planks, praying he didn't see me, praying I'd be safe if I stayed put and waited for him to leave. He took a step toward the truck. The dog strained against the chain, trying to jump out.

"What'd ya hear, boy?" said Snake, reaching for his collar to unclip the chain.

I leapt to my feet and dashed up the staircase. The dog barked in demented, rapid-fire yelps. I reached the top of the cliff just as Snake shouted: "Sic 'em, boy!" and I glanced back to see the dog vaulting over the side of the pickup and scrabbling to the base of the staircase.

I sprinted down the white-stone path to the patio behind the house, leapt the three shallow steps and cut across the flagstones into the forest. Branches slapped my face. Brambles grabbed my legs. I dodged through the obstacle course of tree trunks and jutting rocks. The dog's bark rang clear through the woods. He must have reached the top of the staircase. Ahead of me was the stone pillar. Not far. I could make it.

I pushed my legs into a final sprint. My foot landed crookedly on a tree root. My ankle twisted with a stab of pain. My knee buckled but I caught a branch and stopped myself from falling. Leaves in my face. Where was the pillar? Branches broke behind me as the dog hurtled through the bush.

Two more steps and my hand closed over the cool, rough stone of the pillar. I jammed a foot on a jutting rock and hoisted myself up. The dog burst through the trees and leapt. Its jaws clamped around my ankle. Pain, and the feeling of being wrenched backwards. The skin of my hands scraping against rock as I fell to the ground, kicking. My foot hit something solid. The dog yelped. My ankle came free. I scrabbled to my knees. The dog came at me again, fangs bared. I swung my camera at its head. It jumped back, growling.

"Demon!" called Snake through the woods "Where are you, boy?"

I swung the camera again. The dog dodged, but the camera clipped him on the hindquarters. Demon spun around, leapt on the camera and tackled it to the ground. The strap ripped from my hands. Into Demon's slavering jaws went a thousand bucks' worth of gear and my only proof of the existence of the *Ferox*, but I didn't think twice, turned and scrambled up the pillar.

Snake's voice rang out closer: "Demon! Where are you, boy? Demon!"

Up to the top and jumping down the other side, curling into a ball and rolling as I hit the ground. I stumbled to my feet, the sound of barking close to my ear. The dog hurled itself against the fence, growling and snapping. I took off through the woods, branches whipping my face until I reached the parking lot at last. The sweat stung the scratches on my arms, my cheeks. I flung open the driver's side door.

"You were supposed to lock this!" I screamed at Rhea nonsensically.

"Huh?" Rhea shook herself from a doze.

I floored the gas pedal and went screeching on to the scenic roadway, one eye on the road ahead and one eye in the rearview mirror, watching for Snake's truck behind me.

"What's going on?" said Rhea.

"Grab the map. Find me a turnoff!"

"Where are we?"

"Damned if I know."

"Hayley..."

"Forget it."

I hit the brakes and yanked the wheel around at the sight of a dirt-road turnoff with a sign that said "Kettle's Corners, 12." The Firefly's tires churned up a cloud of dust and pebbles. We crested a hill and disappeared down the other side, out of sight of the scenic roadway. But I didn't stop shaking until we'd passed Kettle's Corners, connected back to the main highway, and merged with the anonymous throng of traffic heading in to Halifax.

Eighteen

I turned my cell on when we hit the city. It was supposedly against the law to talk on the phone while driving, but the five o'clock traffic was so slow, I probably could've gotten off on a legal technicality. Besides, everyone did it.

There was no message from Alex, but Tenzen had left one, so I called him back and we arranged to meet the next day so we could catch up on news. I dropped Rhea off at her place and went home to soak in a hot bath. Dad was working late as usual and I was asleep before he got home, which was a convenient way of avoiding having him question me about what I'd done with my day. Just following a drug dealer and his psycho dog to a lonely spot where no one will ever know what happens to me if I don't return. As an editor, he'd probably be all for it. As a dad, not so much.

The next day, I caught up with Tenzen for lunch at a greasy fish-and-chips joint around the corner from the courthouse. The clientele was a mixture of muscular construction workers in heavy boots and jeans, and slicked-up lawyers raising their cholesterol level it between court appearances. Tenzen didn't fit in with either group, with his coke-bottle glasses and his rumpled brown polyester sports-coat-and-tie combo that looked like he'd bought it out of a Walmart remainder bin.

In front of him on the lunch counter sat the Fisherman's Platter: a crispy heap of fried clams, fried scallops, fried cod, fried zucchini, and French fries. All the bounty of the ocean, drag-netted, breaded, and boiled in oil. Ernest would've had a conniption. I grabbed a stool, snaffled a piece of cod and washed it down with Diet Coke. Ah, civilization.

"So, kiddo, you got something new on the Dervish story?" said Tenzen.

"Yeah," I said. I mowed into the platter and told him all about our high-seas adventure and my recent escapade with Rhea. When I'd finished, he nodded thoughtfully over a forkful of fried clams.

"So, let's recap," he said. "We got a kid, Tyler Dervish, small-time drug dealer, owes money to a bigger-time dealer, guy known as Snake. Dervish goes to meet Snake. Next thing you know, kid's disappeared and his blood's splattered all over a hunting cabin in the woods. Cabin belongs to a guy named something-damned-unpronounceable, otherwise known as Captain Gil. Gil swears he knows nothing about it. Cabin's not locked. Could've been a break-in.

"Act Two: Captain Gil's out on his boat, looking for a giant squid for some nutty school project."

"Turtle," I interrupted him.

"Huh?"

"It was a giant turtle." I hadn't told Tenzen the details of the turtle, or what Dr. Wallis said about it being an undiscovered species. Maybe I didn't have an exclusive on the murder, but at least the living dinosaur was *my* scoop.

"Okay. Giant turtle. Whatever. Point is, another boat appears out of nowhere and someone aboard starts shooting up the place. Name of the boat: *Ferox*.

"Act Three: Back on terra firma. Intrepid reporter-girl follows Snake to a seaside estate. Finds him skulking around a boat. Any old boat? No. The *Ferox.*"

Tenzen held up a fried scallop on his fork.

"Question: What do a drug dealer and a turtle have in common?"

"They're both cold-blooded reptiles," I said.

"True," said Tenzen. "But not relevant. Put it another way. Let's look for connections here. The cabin is connected to Snake *and* to Captain Gil, correct?"

"Correct."

"And the *Ferox* is connected to Snake *and* to Captain Gil, correct?"

"Yeah..."

"So that means that Snake is connected to Captain Gil, correct?"

"Maybe, but..."

"C'mon kiddo, don't give me that six degrees of separation bullshit." He stood up and grabbed his camera from the lunch counter.

"Where are you going?"

"*We're* going," he said, "to talk to Captain Gil."

The address I'd copied from Captain Gil's operating license led to a social housing complex in a semi-industrial neighborhood—a cluster of cracked, narrow sidewalks and boxy brick "garden homes" without much garden. I parked the car and we started down one of the sidewalks, looking for unit 29-B.

There was a playground in the middle of the complex, where a bunch of guys—white, Middle Eastern, black—were playing basketball on a concrete court. The basket had no net and the rim was bent down from guys hot-dogging after slam dunks. In another area of the playground, more dirt than grass, some grade-school kids were kicking around a soccer ball and in one corner, a little black girl—all pretty in a frilly dress with bows in her hair—was skipping rope.

Between the sidewalk and the houses stood a row of scraggly bushes. Used condoms lay in the dirt beneath them. There were probably needles in there, too, but I didn't stop to check. It was a depressing place: the kind of place where single moms and immigrants tried to scrabble out of poverty and raise a family, while pimps and drug dealers tried to drag them down into the muck.

"Not exactly Peggy's Cove," I muttered to Tenzen.

"You said it, kiddo."

We found unit 29-B and Tenzen rang the bell. The woman who answered had a tired face, wrinkles at the corners of her mouth, bleached hair half pulled-back in a slovenly ponytail. She was wearing a pink track suit and smoking a cigarette. Behind her in the living room of the tiny housing unit, a boy was jumping up and down on a beat-up sofa, holding a remote control and flicking through the channels on an old tube TV set, while a toddler in diapers grabbed at his ankles and screamed "Mine! Mine!"

"Sorry to bother you, ma'am." Tenzen stepped forward. "Rod Tenzen, from the *Halifax Independent*. This is Hayley Makk. We're working on a story that involves Captain Gil Chiasson."

"Gil?" She frowned. "He don't live here no more."

She stepped back and made a gesture like she was about to close the door in our faces, when one of the kids let out a bloodcurdling scream, and she spun around.

"Michael, stop it! Oh, Jesus!"

The woman rushed into the living room. The kids were rolling around on the carpet, kicking and biting each other. She dropped to the ground and started pulling them apart with one hand, holding her cigarette in the other. "*Let go of your sister, Michael! I said let go! I swear to God, I'm going to smack the living daylights out of you...*"

"Well," said Tenzen, "I'm outta here."

I turned on him. "What?"

"Boyfriend walked out on her. Last thing she wants is another man around. No way. What she wants a girlfriend to talk to." He thumped me on the shoulder. "That's you, kiddo."

"I'm not her girlfriend."

"Make her think you are."

Tenzen winked and jogged down the stairs and I turned back to the scene in the living room, where the woman had hoisted the boy, kicking and screaming, over her shoulder and was carting him off down a hallway shouting "*Smarten up, Michael! I said, smarten up!*" A second later, a door slammed and the high-pitched wail of a kid getting spanked pierced the thin walls of the housing unit.

I stepped inside.

The toddler was huddled in the corner of the couch, crying. I picked up the remote, sticky with unidentified food remnants, and flicked through the channels until I found a cartoon with some cute animals. I handed the remote to the little girl and she took it warily, like I might've rigged it to explode. After a minute she stopped crying and let me wipe the tears and snot off her face with a semiclean tea towel that I'd found lying on the coffee table. You never knew when that high school babysitting course was going to come in useful.

The woman came back in the room just as I'd gotten the little girl cleaned up.

"Thanks," she said.

"That's okay."

"I shouldn't smoke in front of the kids. Makes them hyper." She picked up her ashtray from the coffee table, moved it to a windowsill, lit another cigarette, and blew the smoke out the window. The gesture didn't do much to improve the indoor air quality. I stood there fiddling with my notepad and pen while she blew more smoke out the window.

"So you're writing about Gil, eh?" she said finally. "Write this down. He's a bastard."

"Why?"

"What else do you call a guy that walks out on two little kids?"

"I didn't know he had kids."

Gil looked way too old to be the dad of those ankle-biters.

"They *think* of him as their father."

Which meant their real dad was God-knows-where.

"He owns that cabin, where Tyler Dervish got beat up," I said. "I know the guys who found it."

"I heard it was a couple of high school kids," the woman said.

I nodded.

"Did you know the other kid, too? Tyler?"

"A little."

"What was he like?" she asked. *Was.*

"He was a creepy kid who wanted to be popular," I said.

She nodded. "There's a lot of those around."

She stood there smoking in silence and I noticed the yellow nicotine stains underneath the chipped pink polish on her fingernails. In the background, the TV cartoon characters sang a song about caring and sharing.

"Everyone thinks Gil done it, because it was his cabin. But he never done it, okay? You can write that down. It was Snake.

Jesus, I told Gil way before, we shoulda just left. Gone out West, y'know? I coulda got a job. But he wouldn't leave Nova Scotia. And now look at this." She gestured at her rundown living room, the food scraps lying on the grubby carpet, the grainy TV set, the uncombed toddler. "It's all Snake's fault. All of it."

Her lips closed in a frown that deepened all the lines on her face: the worry marks on her forehead, the creases that ran from her mouth to her chin.

"What happened?" I said.

She stubbed out her cigarette.

"I'm telling you, but you can't put my name in the paper, 'cause if Snake knew I told you, he'd kill me, okay?"

I nodded, thinking of Snake's depraved pit bull and his voice in the woods, *Sic 'em, boy! Get 'em, Demon!*

"Swear to God," said the woman.

"Swear to God," I said.

She lit another cigarette.

"Okay. It's the middle of the night. Snake comes banging on the door, ringing the bell like he's crazy or tripped out on something. 'Jesus Christ,' I tell him—after I go and open the door—'Jesus Christ, would you shut up? You're gonna wake up the kids.' Snake's not listening, he's all hyper, kicking the walls, shouting for Gil to get out of bed. By this time the baby's crying, so I go into her room to get her back down. That's how come I can hear Snake telling Gil how he just killed some kid down at the cabin. Something about some money he thought the kid owed him, and he just wanted to beat him up, teach him a lesson, and now the kid's dead, and he needs to get rid of the body before the cops find out."

"So Gil says, what the hell's he got to do with getting rid of a body? And Snake says, Gil better help him or else someone's gonna find a dead kid in his cabin, and who's that going to look bad on? And besides, Gil's got a boat."

"What about the *Ferox*?" I said.

"What's the *Ferox*?"

"I thought it was Snake's boat."

If it wasn't, what was Snake doing down at the dock?

"Snake don't have no boat." She shook her head. "No, it was the *Magdelaine*. Gil's boat. So they leave, eh? They take a blanket from the bed to wrap the body in. One of them Hudson's Bay blankets? With the stripes? I was really pissed off. I had that one from my mom. You should see what they cost nowadays.

"Anyways, they left. Gil come back a couple hours later. He was wearing all different clothes and boots. I guess he got rid of the ones, you know...Anyhow, the cops showed up and asked a bunch of questions, but they didn't have nothing on him. Afterwards he packed up his stuff and said he was leaving, and I never seen him after that. He never called, never come back—nothing."

She leaned her forehead against the window.

"I thought he was a decent guy, you know? I mean, he was a fisherman. That's all right. Kind of rough, not super-sensitive, but a good guy. He liked the kids, never made a big deal about how they weren't his, or nothing. Then the government comes along, takes away his fishing license. He wouldn't take another job, eh? Something in the city? That's not him. So then he gets all mixed up with Snake. Goddamned Snake."

"Do you know his real name?" I asked.

She shook her head.

"How did he know Gil?"

"Met him at the docks, I guess. Gil would deliver stuff for him, whenever he needed the money. He just done it for the money. Since the fishery went bust."

"Drugs?" I felt like vomiting.

"Some drugs. Some other stuff. Weird stuff."

She took two paces across the grimy carpet and picked up hamster cage that was perched on a side table crammed with unopened bills. Inside, a little turtle stood with unblinking eyes on a bed of shredded newspaper, amid a scattering of withered apple slices and lettuce leaves.

"What is it?" I said.

"What's it look like? Came from Africa or somewheres. Here, take it." She shoved the cage at my chest and I grabbed it reflexively. "I kept thinking he was going to come back for it, but he ain't coming back. Like I need another mouth to feed."

The TV switched to a talk show and the toddler on the sofa started to cry. The woman went and picked her up, held her close. The little boy came softly out of his bedroom, crept to his mom and started tugging on the hem of her sweatshirt.

"Mommy, mommy, mommy."

"All right, Michael, I'll get you a snack." She turned toward the kitchen, but stopped and looked at me first.

"Swear to God my name never shows up in the paper," she said.

I thought of Snake, and his insane pit bull. She didn't look like Martha Stewart's ideal of mommyhood, but at least she was there for her kids. Which was more than I could say for my mother.

"Swear to God," I said.

Nineteen

I was sitting in the Firefly with the little turtle in its cage beside me, wondering what the hell to do next. What did a drug dealer and a turtle have in common? Make that a drug dealer and two turtles. Tenzen was right. That was more than coincidence.

My cell phone rang and I checked the call display. Unknown number.

"Hayley Makk."

"Hayley. It's Alex Turpin."

Oh, God.

"I tried calling you earlier, but your phone cut out."

"Yeah, hey, sorry about that." I didn't even know whether to call him Alex or Constable Turpin. "I've been having trouble with my network. One of those cheapo plans, you know?"

The lie sounded lame, but he went with it.

"Yeah. I just wanted to make sure you got home safe the other night."

What was I supposed to read into that? That he was interested in me? Or that he was a dutiful officer of the law, serving and protecting the idiotic citizenry?

"I told Trevor he was being a jerk," he added.

"I can take care of myself," I bristled, reverting to porcupine-girl.

Constable Turpin laughed. "So I noticed."

What was he laughing at? Me, a cheap drunk in combat boots and a punked-out kilt? Or Trevor, standing there gob-smacked while his wanna-be-one-night-stand escaped in a cab? I didn't say anything, and the silence hung heavy and awkward on the phone.

"Anyway, I just wanted to check in…"

His voice trailed away in the I'm-gonna-hang-up-now kind of tone.

"Alex?"

"Yeah?"

"Could I…could we, maybe, get together?"

"I'm off shift at seven."

How was that so easy? "No, I mean, it's about Tyler Dervish. The kid, you know…"

"Have you got a lead?"

"Maybe."

"You should be talking to Major Crime. It's Inspector McKay—"

"Alex, I'm not even supposed to be talking to you. My editor would kill me if he knew I was sharing my stuff with the cops, but…"

But I didn't know what else to do. But I couldn't publish a story accusing someone of murder based on unnamed, off-the-record sources. But I was starting to get scared about the connections between Captain Gil, who knew who I was, who knew I'd been asking questions, and Snake, who wouldn't hesitate to get rid of a witness.

"Hang on," said Alex.

I heard his voice, muffled, talking to someone. He got back on the line.

"Half an hour?"

"Sure. Do you remember where I live?"

"I wouldn't forget that, Hayley."

A pulse shot through my chest like a pinball in an arcade game. I said something stupid like "okay, see ya," then shut off the phone and tossed it on the seat next to the turtle cage.

"Alex Turpin," I said to the turtle. It looked at me inscrutably. I revved up the Firefly and headed home.

Half an hour gave me time to shower and change into clean jeans and a t-shirt before I heard the knock on the kitchen door. Constable Turpin had brought his partner Sergeant Beefy along, which was a relief because it kept things on a professional level. I shook hands and invited them to sit down at the kitchen table while I made a pot of tea. I didn't even like tea, but it was a thing you did when people came to the house. Gram always did, anyways. Besides, it gave me something to concentrate on while I tried to stop my mind from replaying scenes of the night at the Midtown. *The crowded sidewalk. Trevor's lips crushing down on mine.*

Sergeant Beefy—whose nametag read Arsenault—went over to inspect the turtle, which was sitting in its cage on the massive chest freezer where Gram stashed the pies and cookies that she baked against the arrival of out-of-town family. Alex Turpin took a seat at the table. Arsenault had a cup of tea but Alex just asked for water. I cracked open a Diet Coke.

"So. Tyler Dervish," said Alex.

"Yeah," I said. "Did you ever hear of a guy named Snake? A drug dealer?"

Sergeant Arsenault grunted.

"Probably a common nickname in the criminal underworld. Why?"

"Someone told me that Tyler was going to meet a guy named Snake. He owed him money. And then, someone else told me that Snake got Captain Gil to help him get rid of Tyler's body."

"Gil Chiasson? The guy who owned the cabin?" said Sergeant Arsenault.

I nodded.

"Investigative reporter, eh?" Sergeant Arsenault said.

I shrugged. "I just found out some stuff."

"Who told you this, Hayley?" said Alex. The way he looked at me distracted me from my job. Something about the look in his brown eyes that was smart and caring without being arrogant, and the forelock that fell in a fringe over his left eyebrow. I steadied myself by looking at Sergeant Arsenault's weather-worn face and his gelled gray hair.

"I can't tell you. It was off the record."

"We may have to subpoena—"

"Drop it," said Sergeant Arsenault. "We don't have time for a court fight." He tapped the turtle cage. "Where'd you get this?"

"Someone gave it to me. They said Captain Gil was supposed to deliver it for Snake."

Sergeant Arsenault nodded.

"Figures."

"What is it?" said Alex.

"What's it look like?"

"A turtle. So what?"

"Tortoise, actually, genius boy. This one's from Madagascar. See those stripes? It's called a radiated tortoise. They're big in the black-market pet trade. Highly illegal."

"How do you know this stuff?"

"I used to work enforcement for the Wildlife Service. You'd be surprised what people will sell on the black market. Eagle feathers. Elephant ivory. Songbirds are big. Lots of animal parts for Chinese medicine. Rhino horns, that kind of stuff. Tortoises, sure, why not? There's a big market for exotic pets. The point is, this guy Snake had a smuggling network set up. And once you've got a network, it doesn't matter what you move along it: drugs, weapons, wildlife. It's all the same to them. It's all product."

"Turtles—" I said.

"Weren't you guys out there looking for a turtle, in the Eastern Islands?" said Alex.

"Yeah. And Ernest got shot when he tried to cut the ne—"

"Probably not a coincidence," said Alex.

"Probably not," I said. "We thought they were just fishermen, but—"

"But what if it was Snake on the *Ferox*?" said Alex.

It made sense, and it explained why I'd seen Snake sneaking around the *Ferox* later on. The boat didn't belong to him, Gil's girlfriend had said, but maybe it belonged to his boss. Or an associate. Or a client.

"So Ms. Cameron hires Captain Gil to help her find this turtle," I said. "He hears her talking about how rare it is. He thinks, great, he can catch it and sell it. He's already connected with Snake's smuggling ring. Only, obviously, he can't be the one catching it, because his boat is full of people. So as soon as we find it, he calls Snake…oh, wait, there was no cell coverage."

"Satellite phone," said Alex.

"Ship's radio," said Sergeant Arsenault.

"Okay. So he calls Snake and tells him where to find it. And pretty soon, Snake shows up in the *Ferox* to catch it. But Ernest cuts the net."

"Which is why Ernest gets shot," said Alex.

"Exactly," I said.

"All right, Holmes and Watson. Brilliant deduction," said Sergeant Arsenault. "Now how much do you want to bet that your captain's out there right now, trying to catch that turtle again?"

"We could find out," I said, remembering the GPS gear that I'd forgotten in the storage compartment beneath my bunk.

I pulled out my laptop and opened it to the webpage that Ms. Cameron and Dr. Wallis had set up to track the turtle's GPS collar. Sure enough, the map on the website showed the Nova Scotia coastline, and a bright dot indicated the location of the GPS transmitter on the *Magdelaine*—heading toward the Eastern Islands. I explained the setup to the cops.

"We should tell Inspector McKay about this," said Alex.

"Now hang on a minute, son," said Sergeant Arsenault. "Inspector McKay is conducting a murder investigation. This is a wildlife-smuggling case."

"But—"

"Of course, if the information we uncovered in a wildlife sting happened to assist in a murder investigation, that could be a good thing for a young cop's career, don't you think?"

"Well—"

"This website got some kind of a password or something?" Sergeant Arsenault turned to me.

"Yeah," I said. "It's confidential. But if you wanted to take me along—"

"I get it. Investigative reporter, eh?"

"It's a great story."

"Okay. All right. You can tag along. But here's the rules: You stay in the background. No interfering with the operation. No talking to witnesses. And you don't report anything until the investigation's over. I don't want to see this all over the Internet."

"Deal," I said. "What about Ms. Cameron and Dr. Wallis? Should we talk to them? I mean—"

"We don't talk to anyone until it's over. Got it?" said Sergeant Arsenault.

"Got it," I said.

"Good," said Sergeant Arsenault. "Here's the deal. I gotta make some phone calls, get some authorizations, work some things out with the Coast Guard. It's late in the day already, and there's no point chasing around after dark, but I'm thinking we want to get out there first thing tomorrow morning. Move fast so we can catch this guy red-handed. That means you need to be ready to go when I call you."

"Okay," I nodded. "Constable Turpin has my cell number."

Sergeant Arsenault turned his steely eyes on Alex, then on me.

"I'll bet he does," he said.

Twenty

My cell rang at six o'clock the next morning.

"We're picking you up in half an hour," Alex said.

I dredged myself out of bed and staggered the window. It was pouring down rain. Apparently, the weather gods had wandered out of the month of July and gotten lost somewhere in mid-October. I dragged on a pair of heavy cargo pants and my Fair Isle sweater, then looked in the mirror. I looked like one of the boys from the bay.

I ditched the outfit for a gray hoodie and a pair of jeans, topped with a thrift-store trench coat. I grabbed my bag and went downstairs to the kitchen.

Dad was sitting at the table, listening to CBC radio and scanning the morning's news headlines on his laptop, while the local TV morning show played in the background.

"How's that story going, Hayley?" he said, without looking up.

I grabbed the two pieces of toast that had just popped out of the toaster.

"Can I eat this?"

"Yeah. Put some more in, would you?"

I reloaded the toaster for Dad and slathered my toast with peanut butter.

"It's going okay, Dad. I got some good pics."

"Write it up today, can you? I need a weekend feature. Then we've got to get you back in the newsroom."

Just like I figured. No matter what he'd said about an A-1 story, dad planned to bury my article in the back pages of the Sunday edition.

"I've got some more reporting to do, Dad. I'm meeting with a cop in a couple of minutes."

"A cop?" Dad looked up from his computer. "I thought this was a science story, Hayley."

"Yeah, it turned out to be more complicated than that."

Out the window, I spotted the police cruiser pulling up to the curb.

"I gotta go."

"Hayley!" Dad shouted in his editor-in-chief voice. I stopped and turned around.

"Text me a skedline. I want to know where you're at and what's going on."

"Yeah, Dad."

I pulled up my gray cotton hood and made a dash for the cruiser, splashing through the water that ran down the driveway. Alex leaned over and opened a door to the backseat. He was riding shotgun while Sergeant Arsenault sat behind the wheel.

"You're going to get soaked," he said as I climbed in.

"I'll be okay."

"You need a rain hat," said Alex. "We'll get you one at the Coast Guard station."

I didn't need guys taking care of me, but he had a point, so I kept my mouth shut.

Nobody said much as we wove through the streets toward the highway, the windshield wipers swiping maniacally at the driving rain.

We left the city behind and hit the highway toward Tangier. Halifax's stunted suburbs gave way to forest. The rain continued beating down. The air inside the car became warm and humid. The police radio crackled with routine calls and communications with the Coast Guard station in Tangier that Alex or his partner would take, giving Trevor updates on our ETA and discussing the position of the *Magdelaine* according to the website, which Alex had pulled up on a laptop that was fastened to the cruiser's console. Just as we'd suspected, Captain Gil was puttering around Black Duck Island.

I leaned my forehead against the window. The pane made a cold spot on my skin. I tried not to think about that night in the bar with Trevor-Forever, and how I'd made a total fool of myself. I wondered if maybe I should talk to Alex about it some time. Maybe explain to him about how having a mom who ran out on me as a baby made me so paranoid about getting involved with guys. But I didn't think I wanted him to know all that stuff about me, about my past and my mother. I didn't want him to see me as some troubled teenager who needed his help. No, he was a cop. And I was a reporter chasing a story. And the less personal it got between us, the better.

A call came over the radio from Tangier, Trevor's voice crackling through the static:

"He's moving. west. Away from the islands. Where are you guys?"

Sergeant Arsenault picked up the radio handset.

"Five minutes ETA," he said. "Get ready to roll."

The rain was still pouring down when we turned off the highway and bumped down the steep, gravel road through the woods that led to the Tangier Coast Guard Station. At the bottom of the hill lay the flat, open area where the ambulance had stood waiting for us that night after Ernest was shot. Now, instead of the commotion and the strobing red emergency light, there were only a few seagulls scavenging for scraps and the deserted wharf stretching into the gray blur of rain on seawater.

A few meters from the bottom of the hill, Sergeant Arsenault pulled over into a leveled-off parking area beside the Coast Guard building. I hadn't noticed the station last time, but then it wasn't exactly a stunning piece of modern architecture: a gray, concrete box with a satellite dish stuck to one side and a radio antenna jutting from the roof. A red Maple Leaf and a blue Coast Guard ensign hung limply on a flagpole outside.

"Let's go," said Alex. I slung my bag over my shoulder and followed the cops through the mud and gravel parking lot.

Inside the Coast Guard building, the decor lived up to the exterior's utilitarian-institutional motif. Radio and computer equipment crammed the single room, with tide-tables, weather bulletins, and navigational charts taped to the cinder-block walls. The place smelled of wet clothes and strong coffee.

Trevor was sitting at a gray metal table in front of a computer screen, eating something greasy out of a McDonald's wrapper and drinking coffee from an Irving Big Stop mug. The minute I saw him, I felt a wave of anger and nausea—an urge to slap his face, mixed with a shamefaced impulse to slink away and hide. I pulled out a notepad instead and started writing down some observations about the station. Act professional, Hayley.

"About time you guys got here," Trevor said. He turned to me.

"Hello, sweetheart," he winked. Unbelievable.

"Down, boy," growled Sergeant Arsenault. "None of that on my watch. Let's go over the plan."

He pulled out a tablet computer set to the website that showed the *Magdelaine*'s GPS position. He walked over to a nautical chart tacked to a wall and stuck his finger on it.

"Okay, our boy's here."

He moved his finger to Tangier.

"And we're here."

He drew his finger up the coastline and stopped at a narrow peninsula, shaped like a hook.

"So far, he's been following the coastline. It's rough weather out there, so when he gets around this point of land, he'll want to tuck in here, into the lee. Now there's a little island, right here. We wait for him behind the island. Once he comes around the bend, we come out this way and intercept him."

"Hang on," Trevor interrupted. "Why don't we just track him and wait till he comes ashore? It's easier to confront him on dry land."

"Too risky," Sergeant Arsenault said. "We don't know where he's coming ashore. It might be someplace we don't want a confrontation."

"It's risky at sea," Trevor argued. "What if he dumps the goods overboard? Then we've got no evidence."

"Not so easy to dump a whacking big turtle," said Sergeant Arsenault.

"Okay, what if he makes a run for it?"

"Alex says this boat of his looked like it couldn't outrun a well-manned dory. Besides, we'll have him cornered." Sergeant Arsenault tapped the map and continued. "Right. We take a friendly approach. It's a routine fishing patrol. If there's nothing suspicious, it's 'Thank you Captain, have a pleasant day.' If he's got the sea turtle, we take our plan from there."

Alex nodded.

"What is the plan?" I whispered to him.

He made a little 'have-patience' motion with his hand, but didn't answer.

"You got the gear, Alex?"

"Yeah," he held up a black case.

"Right," said Sergeant Arsenault. "Let's go."

The three guys shrugged on heavy Coast Guard raincoats that were hanging by the door. I shoved my notepad in an inside pocket and followed them. Alex lifted a black rain hat from a hook on the wall and stuck it on my head. He yanked the brim down over my eyes. Very funny.

I pushed the brim back. Alex was heading out the door.

"I still don't know what the plan is," I said.

"Don't worry," said Alex. "At least you won't get wet."

Trevor took the helm of the Canadian Coast Guard Ship *Joshua Slocum*, while Sergeant Arsenault slotted his notepad computer into a holder by the co-pilot's seat and hooked it up to a cable.

"Won't we lose the signal out there?" said Alex.

"We've got sat," Trevor replied. "Besides, he'll show up on the ship's radar pretty soon." He nodded toward a screen beside him.

Trevor set the boat in motion, picking up speed as we left the cove. The guys started talking to each other in nautical law-enforcement jargon that I didn't understand, and wasn't supposed to. Still, I took out my notepad and jotted down some quotes. Maybe I could use it for color. Maybe Alex would decipher it for me later. Maybe I just wanted to feel like I was doing something useful, rather than sitting there huddled in my trench coat.

The rain continued pelting down. The *Slocum* pitched and heaved through the choppy waves. The more Trevor drove the boat forward, the more the ocean tried to fling it sideways against the rocks. Finally, we arrived at a sheltered cove and the pitching stopped as we motored toward the so-called island that Sergeant Arsenault had picked for our ambush. It wasn't much more than a couple of rocks topped by scrubby pines, but at least it provided some cover, which we badly needed. The *Slocum* had a bright red hull and a gleaming white pilot-house, decorated with the red maple-leaf logo. It looked like a floating Canada-Day cake. Great for patriotism, not so hot when it came to camouflage, if you asked my opinion. But then, no one was asking my opinion.

"Not much time to spare," Sergeant Arsenault said.

I stood up and looked over their shoulders. The dot that represented the *Magdelaine* was now visible on the ship's radar screen, working its way along the jagged line that represented the coast. The dot reached the base of the peninsula and continued around the curving hook, until it rounded the point. I looked out the windshield. Through the screen of the pine trees and the driving rain, an indistinct shape moved towards us.

"Let's get him," said Trevor.

"Wait," said Sergeant Arsenault. "Wait."

We waited as the *Magdelaine* moved further into the cove, waited until the curve of the peninsula cut off her escape route to the open sea. Waited longer as the boat approached the island.

"Now!"

Trevor gunned the motor and raced around the island. He hit a burst on the siren and flashed the red emergency light. Captain Gil's fishing boat lit up in the scarlet glare.

Sergeant Arsenault stepped on deck.

"Ahoy, *Magdelaine*! Come alongside!"

But the instinct of Gil's rum-running ancestors must have kicked in, because his boat bucked, threw up a wake of spray, and sped into the narrow channel between the island and the coast.

"Damn!" yelled Trevor.

He yanked the wheel around. The *Slocum* spun on a dime. I staggered back against the wall. Felt my feet slip out from under me. Flung out a hand for something to hold on to. Felt a hand grab me, steady me. Alex. The boat cleared the point of the island just as Gil came around the other side. If Trevor hadn't intercepted him, he would have had a clear run out to sea. Instead, our boat forced Gil to hug the coastline. Trevor sped toward him, angling his course, crowding the *Magdelaine*, cutting it off, edging it closer to the jagged rocks of the shore.

The rain drove into the pilothouse. The wind whipped the ends of my trench coat. We sped along the coastline to the end of the sheltered cove. Around the point, the waves hit us full force. We crashed and jolted like a truck on a rutted back-road.

"Come alongside, Captain!" Sergeant Arsenault bellowed.

It was a game of chicken that Gil couldn't win. He had no room to maneuver—no space to turn around, and not enough speed to dart ahead and cut in front of us. Still, he didn't give up.

"Crazy fool," said Alex.

"I knew this was going to happen," Trevor muttered through gritted teeth.

He pressed a button and a loudspeaker sent his voice booming into the air.

"Ahoy, Captain! Submerged rocks ahead! Come around!"

The *Slocum* swerved to avoid a rock. The *Magdelaine* swerved but not in time and its hull scraped with a sickening sound against a rock. Gil cut the boat's engine to a putter and she floated, suddenly docile.

Trevor swung around and pulled alongside of him.

"Are you all right, Captain?" Sergeant Arsenault called.

"Dented my hull, *hostie*. Lucky it didn't tear a hole in her."

"Fishing patrol, Captain. Mind if we come aboard?"

"Can't stop you, can I?"

I trailed Alex and Sergeant Arsenault aboard the *Magdelaine* while Trevor stayed back in the pilothouse. Gil stood defiantly on deck, the hood of his oil slicker pushed back, the rain beating on his deeply weathered face. The boat's hold was filled by the massive body of the sea turtle. Entangled in Gil's net, the turtle looked pathetic. Its head was wedged into a corner. Its flippers stuck out over the edges.

"That's some catch you've got there, Captain," said Sergeant Arsenault.

"Come up in my net. I was fishing for turbot," said Gil.

"You have a license for turbot, do you Captain?"

"Used to. Government took it away," he mumbled. "How's a man supposed to make a living?"

"Fishing without a license. That's a serious offense," said Sergeant Arsenault, as though he was on a mission to nail every turbot poacher from Yarmouth to Chedabucto.

"Didn't catch any, did I?"

"No. Looks like you caught something else, though," Sergeant Arsenault said. "You're aware, are you Captain, that trading in marine reptiles is an offense under the Wild Animal and Plant Protection and Regulation Act?"

"I ain't trading nothing. I told you, it come up by accident," said Gil. "I never seen one like it. I was taking it to Halifax, for scientific identification."

Scientific identification. You had to admire the guy's nerve.

"Is that right?" said Sergeant Arsenault.

"Ain't illegal."

"No. But helping a murderer dispose of a dead body—that would be illegal, wouldn't you say, Captain?"

Gil's face gave nothing away. "Imagine it would be."

"What if I told you that I have a witness who'll swear they saw you and a drug dealer by the name of Snake, loading something that looked like a dead body aboard this very boat?"

Gil's hands clenched and unclenched.

"I'd say I don't know what the hell you're talking about."

"Captain, I can have this boat impounded. I can swab every square inch of it for DNA. A hair. A fingernail. A tiny spot of blood. That's all it takes. Do you know the penalty for accessory after the fact to murder? Life in prison, Captain. Life."

Gil stood as rigid as ever, but doubt weakened the defiance in his eyes. Like the turtle, he was trapped, his hard shell useless as a defense.

"What do you boys want?" Gil glared at me. "She's with the newspaper."

"We don't have to talk in front of her," said Sergeant Arsenault. "Come on up to the pilothouse, Captain. Where we can have a private chat."

Sergeant Arsenault gripped Gil's shoulder and they climbed the ladder to the pilothouse. Alex turned to follow them.

"Alex!" I hissed. He looked back at me.

"Sorry, Hayley. Go on below and get out of the rain."

Twenty-one

"What's going on?" I asked Alex again, when he came down to the galley a long time later.

I'd taken shelter against the rain in its grimy familiarity. The stained ceramic mugs in the sink might have been the same ones that Ms. Cameron and I had drunk tea from on the trip back to Tangiers three days ago. The foul, feral smell of Ernest's dirty wool poncho hung faintly in the air. A gray murk of rain and spray shrouded the view from the porthole, as the *Magdelaine* plodded toward and unknown location. Alex lit the gas stove and put a kettle on to boil.

"I can't talk to you about it, Hayley. Sorry. My partner's in charge of media relations."

"Media relations?" I said. "Your partner's idea of media relations is 'no comment.'"

Alex smiled, and it made him so good-looking that I had to turn away before I started thinking about the fact that the two of us were alone in a dimly lit room. Thinking like that wasn't going to get me a story.

"He says he'll give you a debriefing later," Alex added.

Right. A debriefing later. I'd fallen for that one before. And one thing I'd learned was, if you want the story, get as much information as you can, whenever you can, from whoever you can. Never wait for the debriefing later.

"Forget this debriefing stuff, Alex. Arsenault's not going to tell me anything. You know what Arsenault's going to say? He's going to say the RCMP is 'pursuing a number of leads' and 'speaking to persons of interest' but it 'cannot divulge operational details at this time due to the ongoing nature of the investigation.' That's what Arsenault's going to say. Right?"

Alex didn't answer.

"Right?"

Alex took the kettle off the stove and poured two mugs of tea.

"Yeah. You're probably right."

"So?"

Alex carried the tea to the table and sat down. He pushed one mug over to me.

"Sugar?"

"Yeah, thanks."

I heaped sugar in my tea and waited.

"Okay, look, I'll tell you what's going on, but don't quote me in the paper, okay?"

"Okay."

"I could get in a lot of trouble, Hayley."

"I never burn my sources, Alex."

I held his eyes. I wanted him to know that he could trust me. That I took my job and his job seriously. That I wasn't some cheap tabloid paparazza who'd blow his trust for the sake of a screaming headline.

He nodded.

"Okay. First of all, he's not admitting anything about the murder."

"Figures."

"Yeah. But we got him to admit that that catching that monster turtle wasn't exactly a coincidence. He's meeting with this guy, Snake, and they're going to sell it to a buyer up the coast. Some kind of exotic pet fanatic."

"So what are you going to do?"

"Gil's agreed to wear a wire. Ideally, we get enough evidence on the record to charge Snake with trading in restricted wildlife."

"What about the murder?"

"That's the end-game, Hayley. Once we charge Snake, we get fingerprints. Maybe a DNA sample. We match that to evidence from the murder scene. Plus, we get access to his records. Phone logs. Emails. There may be trail of messages leading up to his meeting with the victim, Tyler Dervish."

"Sounds good," I said.

"Yeah, if it works."

"What about the turtle?"

Alex shrugged.

"What about it?"

"What happens to it, in the end?"

"I don't know. Maybe it ends up in a zoo somewhere."

"It should go back in the ocean. Ms. Cameron says it's really rare." I couldn't believe it: I sounded like Ernest. Save the sea turtles. Free the whales.

"I don't know, Hayley," Alex repeated. "This is a murder investigation. It's about nailing a killer. What happens to the wildlife isn't exactly at the top of everyone's mind."

Nailing a killer. And Snake wasn't just a killer. He was a guy who dealt drugs to teenagers. The red needle-mark on the inside of Rhea's arm. *I gave blood. Okay?* Did she? Or did Snake get her into the hard stuff, that night at the party? Why should the turtle pay for all that? It had its own life, unchanged for millions of years. The creature had no idea it was caught up the crazy schemes of humans. I didn't say that out loud, though. Alex would have thought I'd gone loony.

Alex finished his tea and stood up.

"I gotta go back."

"Alex..."

"I can't give you anything more right now."

I watched as he turned his back to me and became an anonymous figure in a dark raincoat and heavy boots that climbed the ladder and disappeared. I waited a few minutes and made my way on deck.

The rain was still pouring down. The waves beat monotonously against the endless rocks of the coastline. There was no one on deck except me. And the sea turtle. I sat down beside her.

"Sorry, sister," I said out loud. Her yellow eyes, set deep in her bald, bony head, blinked back at me. I reached my index finger through a hole in the net and stroked her hide. It felt rough, like old leather. At least she was taking her ordeal stoically—or maybe there just wasn't much going on in her pint-sized, prehistoric brain.

I moved my finger to trace the starburst pattern on her shell. I could see how someone would want to collect her: like a sculpture or a precious stone, forgetting she was a living thing. Was Alex any better, sacrificing her to entrap Snake? Was I any better, standing by and letting him do it?

I stood up. The net that held the sea turtle was attached to a heavy cable, which was drawn over a pulley and wrapped around a winch in the stern. I grabbed the crank that turned the winch and pulled. I couldn't raise her an inch. Maybe if Ernest had been here we could have mounted a joint rescue operation. Me and Ernest, fighting together for environmental justice—what a joke. Besides, did I really want to sabotage Alex's investigation? Ruin the chance to bust Snake's smuggling ring? Give a murderer an opportunity to walk free?

I sat down on the deck next to Nyota. The rain streamed down my trench coat collar.

"Sorry, sister," I said again. "There's nothing I can do."

Twenty-two

"Get below," Sergeant Arsenault snapped.

He waved me toward the hatch and followed me down the ladder, heavy boots creaking on the rungs above my head, raincoat dripping cold water on my hands.

Down in the galley, Alex was fiddling with the ship's radio, rigging it to receive and record the transmissions from Captain Gil's wire.

"How much longer?" he asked his partner.

"Captain says about ten minutes." Sergeant Arsenault tossed his rain hat on the counter. "Are we ready?"

"Yeah. It's working."

I slid on to the bench and peered out the porthole. As we rounded the point into the next cove, I had a strange feeling that I knew the place, but couldn't identify it. Then I realized that it was only a change in perspective: Last time, I'd seen the cove from the high shore above. Now I was looking at it from sea level. But the landmarks were the same—the wooden staircase zigzagging up the bluff; the concrete boat-launch, the gravel road leading up through a cut in the cliff, the dock with the boat tied to it, a white boat with a blue stripe. The

Ferox. The only things missing were Snake and his nutso pit bull. I had a feeling they might not be far away.

"Hayley, get away from the porthole," Alex said.

The galley was so dim I doubted anyone ashore could have seen inside. Still he was probably right. We couldn't risk someone glimpsing a suspicious shape or movement, anything that might hint there were more people aboard than just Captain Gil. God knows what would happen if anything went wrong in a situation where a guy double-crossed his criminally violent boss. As Anne of Green Gables might have said, there was lots of scope for the imagination.

Who owned the mansion at the top of the hill? Was it Snake? Or was it the buyer—some wealthy eccentric who collected rare animals as a warped hobby? Is that why Snake had come here, when I'd followed him the day before? Was he setting up the deal with the buyer? He could've done it by phone, but maybe he was afraid the cops were bugging his line. Who was the buyer, anyway? I thought about the gun that I'd seen, leaning against the desk in the room behind the French doors. If this got ugly, it could get ugly fast.

The boat slowed down, drifted for a few moments and jolted backward. The stench of diesel filled the galley and the motor churned in reverse as the captain maneuvered the *Magdelaine* alongside the wharf. Finally, he cut the motor. His heavy boots creaked across the deck and stepped on to the wharf, where he'd be tying the boat to its mooring. Through the radio, we heard him muttering to himself in indecipherable Acadian. Arsenault nodded. The transmission system was working. So far, so good. Now all we could do was wait. And listen.

At first we heard only static, punctuated by the huffing of Captain Gil's breath. He'd be climbing the zigzag staircase, a steep course of frequent switchbacks up the sheer cliff. Close by, waves slapped against the boat's hull and the rain continued its steady, monotonous patter on the deck above our heads.

Alex slid on to the bench beside me.

"I know this place," I whispered.

He looked at me and raised his eyebrows.

"I followed Snake here. There's a gravel path at the top of the staircase."

"Shhh!" Sergeant Arsenault glared from across the room.

I shut my mouth but soon, as though to prove me right, we heard a rhythmic crunch-crunch-crunch—the sound of heavy boots treading on gravel.

Alex took my notepad and wrote on it:

What's at the end of the path?

A mansion. I wrote back. *Don't know who lives there. I saw a gun.*

Alex's thigh touched mine. A warmth spread through my leg that was more than just his body heat. Why did he do that? Reassurance? Coincidence? I shot a glance at him, but he was looking over at Arsenault.

I forced myself to focus on the task at hand.

The sound of Gil's footsteps and his heavy breathing filled the galley. I could picture him tramping through the woods, stone-faced, oblivious to the rain dripping from the canopy of trees. All at once the sound of his footsteps changed, became more solid, and I guessed he had stepped off of the gravel footpath on to the stone terrace behind the mansion.

A gruff voice came through the radio:

"You got it?"

Captain Gil answered:

"Down at the boat."

"Is it alive?"

"Is for now. Can't say for how long."

"Why?" The voice sharp and threatening. "Is something wrong?"

"Shouldn't take them creatures from the ocean, is all."

"God, another fucking tree-hugger."

More sounds crackled through the radio—rustling, footsteps—then another voice, slow and wheezy:

"Don't worry, Captain. You can rest assured that your turtle will be well taken care of."

That voice. I knew it.

"Doctor Wallis," I whispered.

"Who?" Alex turned to me.

"Doctor—"

"Shush!" Sergeant Arsenault cut us off with a brusque hand-motion.

"Are you certain it's the right one?" wheezed Dr. Wallis. "Are you certain it will fit in the truck?"

"We'll make 'er fit," came the voice that must be Snake's. "Come on. Get in."

Sergeant Arsenault shut off the radio's speaker, snapping my mind from the scene on the terrace back to the dim, cramped galley.

"They're coming down," he said. "Get in there."

He looked at me and jerked his head toward the small door that led to the cabin in the bow.

"No way. I'm staying here."

"Hayley, it's not safe," said Alex. "We don't have time to argue about this."

"I'm getting this story, Alex."

"Fine. Get under the table."

"Under…?"

"Just do it."

I slithered to the cold floor, my head bent beneath the tabletop, my notepad propped on one cramped thigh. Sergeant Arsenault pulled the hatch shut. Alex joined him, standing on the other side of the ladder that led up to the deck. He shrugged off his raincoat and loosened the service gun in its holster at his hip

The grinding of tires on gravel signaled Harman's truck pulling up outside. Car doors slammed and boots creaked on the wharf, then on the deck overhead. Alex drew his gun. Sergeant Arsenault left his in its holster. I couldn't decide which made me feel less safe.

"There she is, Doc. Take a look." Snake's voice was coarse and boastful. And close. Too close.

The professor's deep, wheezy voice answered:

"Unbelievable. It's…it's fantastic."

"Just get 'er on the truck," said Captain Gil. "Tide'll be turning. I ain't got all day."

"No, of course…" Dr. Wallis' voice trailed off in a fit of coughing, then came his feeble wheeze: "Captain, if you might have a glass of water…"

Footsteps creaked overhead. Alex and Sergeant Arsenault drew themselves flat against the wall, into the shadows where they couldn't be seen from someone on deck, looking down the hatch. The hatch door swung open.

Captain Gil climbed down slowly, unhurried. He frowned at Alex's gun, turned and caught sight of me crouched beneath the table. I felt like an illegal Mexican, crossing the American border in the back of a bogus delivery truck, with Captain Gil the bought-off customs inspector paid to turn a blind eye. The captain grunted and filled a glass of water from the sink. Through the hatch, I could see two pairs of boots on deck, and the silver tip of Dr. Wallis' cane. Gil climbed out and closed the hatch. I tried to breathe normally, but my heart hammered so hard I could feel the buzz from my ribcage to my skull.

Doctor Stanford Wallis. The renowned biologist. Ms, Cameron's mentor. No wonder he'd been so interested in her fieldwork. He was the one who'd helped her to hire Captain Gil's boat. He was the one who'd given her the GPS tracking equipment. It was obvious he'd never meant to support her scientific research. All along, he'd been scheming together with Captain Gil and Snake to capture the sea turtle and keep it for himself. And if he was a client of Snake's, the scheme might be bigger than just one animal. I thought of the little tortoise in the cage, and wondered if it, too, was meant to have gone to Dr. Wallis.

Above decks, the winch ratcheted and groaned. What did Dr. Wallis intend to do with the turtle? Sell it? Keep it alive? My mind flashed back to the pond with the moss-covered fountain, in the rose garden beside the patio at the back of the mansion. Would that be the turtle's new home? Or did Dr. Wallis intend to stuff it and mount it like a gruesome object d'art? Did he know about the drug-dealing? Was he part of that, too?

Truck doors slammed shut. An engine growled. Gravel crunched beneath tires—first nearby, then fainter. When the sound of the truck faded into the white noise of waves and rain, Alex lowered his gun and fell into the chair beside the radio.

"Shit," he said.

Sergeant Arsenault flipped the speaker back on.

I crawled out from under the table.

"You okay?" Alex said.

"Yeah. Alex, that was Dr. Wallis. I'm sure of it."

"Who?"

"The guy with the wheezy voice. The buyer. It was Dr. Stanford Wallis."

"Who's Dr. Stanford Wallis?" said Sergeant Arsenault.

"A professor at the university. He was the one who sent Ms. Cameron to look for the turtle in the first place."

"You can't trust anyone," muttered Arsenault.

"Must be what Captain Gil meant by 'scientific identification.'" Alex's voice was bitter.

"That's what they'll argue in court," said Sergeant Arsenault. "And at this point they'd get away with it. We haven't got a crime until money changes hands."

He turned up the volume on the radio and meaningless static filled the cabin, until the sound of Dr. Wallis' voice came through.

"Turn to the left here. There's a pond in the rose garden. You can drive the truck on to the terrace. Yes, here. The gate's a little rusty, but I think once we get it open, we can back the truck up to the pond. If you could help me open the gate, Captain..."

Doors slammed, followed by the sound of footsteps. I could picture them walking on the terrace behind the mansion, where just two days before I'd crouched in the bushes, trying to catch a glimpse of Snake through the heavy curtains that shrouded the patio doors.

There were metallic sounds of clanging and grating, as though someone were trying to fit a key into an old iron lock. Just then another voice broke through the radio. A woman's voice.

"Dr. Wallis!"

"Who's that?" Sergeant Arsenault leaned toward the radio.

I didn't have time to say anything before Dr. Wallis replied:

"Nora, my dear. What a pleasure to see you. What brings you here in this terrible weather?"

Ms. Cameron.

"I've been trying to reach you," she said. "You said you'd get in touch about continuing the expedition. But you didn't return my phone calls. I was worried something had happened. I know your health hasn't been good."

"I'm terribly sorry, Nora. I've merely been busy. Preoccupied. Please, come inside. You must be perished."

"I wanted to talk to you about the turtle. I'm sorry, I didn't know you had visitors. Captain Gil and..."

"Yes, yes, the good captain." Dr. Wallis gave a phlegmy, forced laugh. "But do come inside, Nora. I'll put the kettle on."

"I parked around front. I rang the bell but there was no answer so I came looking and I heard voices out back here."

"Yes, yes, but do come inside. You'll catch your death of cold." I pictured him trying to escort her into the mansion through the French doors that led off of the terrace. Keeping up the pretense of the gentlemanly old professor, while just behind him in the pickup truck, the turtle sat like a thousand-pound hunk of incriminating evidence.

Alex stood up.

"We should go in," he said.

His partner stopped him with a hand on his shoulder.

"Wait. We got nothing. No transaction. No crime."

"There's a civilian on scene. She could get hurt."

"Settle down," said Sergeant Arsenault. "He's inviting her in for tea. Wait and see what happens."

"We can't risk it," said Alex.

"We can't risk missing the chance to nail this bastard."

They stared at one another, Alex gripping the ladder, Sergeant Arsenault gripping Alex's shoulder.

A voice crackled through the radio—a high-pitched shout, like the cry of a protester at a social justice rally.

"Ms. Cameron! They've got Nyota!"

Holy shit. Ernest.

"Who the hell's that?" Sergeant Arsenault whipped around to face the radio as though he could see through it to the scene at the mansion above. I could picture it all perfectly: that huge mansion surrounded by forest, with the truck parked on the back terrace beside the rose garden with its marble nymph perched on the top of her fountain, looking down at the bizarre scene. On the terrace, Dr. Wallis trying to escort Ms. Cameron through the French doors into the mansion. Snake and Captain Gil standing somewhere nearby. And now, Ernest.

"Ernest. The kid who got shot," I said.

"Come and look, Ms. Cameron! She's in the truck!"

"We're going in," said Alex.

"Call Trevor first. Get some backup."

Alex grabbed a cell phone.

"The battery's dead on this thing."

Snake's voice broke through the static:

"Get away from my truck, kid."

"I won't!"

"Get back from there, Ernest!" shouted Ms. Cameron. "Dr. Wallis, what's going on?"

"Come inside, Nora. We'll talk..."

"I won't come inside until you explain to me..."

"You heard him lady. Get the fuck inside."

"Don't do it Ms. Cameron! They're going to kidnap her!"

"Kid, I said, get the hell away from my truck!"

Alex swung on to the ladder and burst through the hatch. Sergeant Arsenault followed. I scrambled up behind them, into the pelting rain, vaulted off the boat and onto the slippery planks of the wharf. I skidded, fell to one knee. Ahead, Alex and his partner had already reached the zigzag staircase.

I made it to the bottom of the staircase and grabbed the handrail, took the stairs two by two. How far to the top? I couldn't remember the number of switchbacks. A gull screeched in my face, wheeling on an updraft. The rain beat down.

Another landing. Another switchback. Boots thudded above me. The staircase shook. I gripped the handrail, slick with rain. *Don't fall.* I turned another switchback. The end of the staircase loomed above. The two cops had already reached the platform. They took off down the path, guns drawn. I climbed faster, lungs searing, thighs burning, rain soaking down my collar. Wind howled off the sea-bluff. At last, the platform. I took off down the path through the woods. Tree branches creaked and groaned. A million leaves rattled. A crack split the air. I ducked: A tree branch, brought down by the wind, I thought.

Then: No, not a tree branch.

A gunshot.

Twenty-three

"Police! Drop your weapon!" Sergeant Arsenault's voice shouted as I burst out of the woods onto the terrace behind Dr. Wallis' mansion. Light streamed from the open patio doors. Alex and Sergeant Arsenault stood rigid, guns pointed at a figure on the terrace. A tall, gaunt figure holding a hunting rifle.

Dr. Wallis.

Slowly, slowly, he lowered the rifle and let it clatter to the ground. He staggered backwards, raising his hands as though groping for something to steady himself. Ms. Cameron rushed to his side.

"Don't shoot!" she called. "He saved our lives."

I turned to look in the direction where Dr. Wallis' rifle had pointed. There on the flagstones beside the pickup truck, lay the drug dealer Snake. He was face-up on the ground and a dark stain spread over his chest. A handgun lay on the ground beside his outstretched arm as though it had been flung from his grasp as he fell. Ernest was slumped against the back of the pickup truck. Rain poured down his face, his t-shirt, his faded hemp pants. I went over and touched his arm. It felt cold and clammy.

"Are you okay?"

He stared at me with shell-shocked eyes.

"Nyota," he said.

"You saved her," I said. "Twice."

There were goose bumps on his arm and he was starting to shake. I took off my trench coat and wrapped it around him. As I did, my phone fell out of the pocket. I picked it up and—even though it felt wrong—I took a couple shots of the scene. Snake's body on the ground. Dr. Wallis hunched in Ms. Cameron's arms. Dad would expect photos. A reporter's job is to bear witness, he'd said often enough. Now it felt like a weak pretext for disturbing a scene of raw grief.

"Alex, get the media out of here," shouted Sergeant Arsenault.

A hand touched my shoulder.

"Come on, Hayley," he said. "Come inside."

He led me across the terrace. Past the forms of Dr. Wallis and Ms. Cameron, huddled together in the beating rain. Past Captain Gil, standing to one side with his arms crossed over his chest as though none of this had anything to do with him. Through the wide-open patio doors and into the study.

It was decorated in the manner of British colonial splendor: carved wooden furniture; intricate Indian rugs; red velvet window draperies that fell from ceiling-high rods and puddled in heaps of excess fabric on the floor. I recognized the ornate fireplace I'd glimpsed through the gap in the curtains two days before, when I'd followed Snake here. The massive wooden desk, no rifle leaning against it now. The rifle had been used to kill a man.

Ceiling-to-floor bookshelves lined every wall. They were filled not with books, but with glass aquariums of many sizes. A stench of urine and rotting food rose from the aquariums, and their interiors could only be dimly glimpsed through a film of dirt and grime. Some were landscaped like miniature deserts of sand and pebbles, with heat-lamps burning above of them. Others were made to simulate ponds—half water, half artificial shoreline of wood, stone, dirt and plants, their glass coated in green algae. Inside the aquariums, dozens of turtles poked listlessly at scraps of moldy fruit and withered lettuce leaves.

I took another step and nearly tripped over an oversized footstool. The footstool raised its head and looked back at me. It was a giant tortoise.

It seemed Dr. Wallis had imported half the Galapagos as home decor.

"We better call the Wildlife Service on this one," Alex muttered.

"Good Lord, Dr. Wallis," came Ms. Cameron's voice from behind me. "Good Lord."

I turned. Ms. Cameron and Dr. Wallis had just entered the room, followed by Sergeant Arsenault and Ernest. Dr. Wallis was leaning heavily on Ms. Cameron's arm. She helped him to a chair before stepping away from him.

"My collection, Nora," Dr. Wallis' voice shook. "My life's work, since I left the University."

A fit of coughing interrupted the old man's speech. Ms. Cameron hesitated whether to go to him. Before she could decide he recovered, straightened up.

"Please forgive the...shabby condition, Nora. I am growing too old to care for them all."

Ms. Cameron looked sick to her stomach.

"Dr. Wallis, surely, these are endangered species..."

"Many of them. That's why...That's how..." the old man faltered. "How do I explain to you, Nora? I had to take extraordinary measures...I tried to go through the proper channels. But, the bureaucrats wouldn't bend or budge. They didn't understand why I needed them. I needed them! I am a scientist, not a criminal! Even Charles Darwin had…a collection. Even Darwin…"

He bowed his head and crumpled from his shoulders down, until he was completely bent over, elbows on his knees, face in his hands.

Ms. Cameron stepped toward him. She put her hand on his shoulder.

"You saved our lives."

Sergeant Arsenault stepped forward.

"I'll place a call to headquarters. Then I'll need witness statements. Alex, get the media out of here."

Alex touched my arm and I moved close to him. I had a dozen more questions I wanted to ask Dr. Wallis, but Alex shot me a warning glance and steered me out the door to a dusty formal dining room.

"Stay here, Hayley, okay?" He squeezed my arm then let it go. "I'll come and get you when it's time to head home."

"Can I interview Dr. Wallis?"

"No."

"Are you going to charge him?"

"You never give up, do you Hayley?"

"It's my job, Alex."

He looked away from me, at the rain beating against the leaded panes of the old-fashioned window.

"Sergeant Arsenault's in charge of media relations," he said.

"Come on, Alex."

"Sorry, Hayley. I gotta go."

He turned away.

"I have to file a story."

"Now?" He looked back at me.

"A man's dead, Alex. It's a big story. It's going to get out anyhow. You'll have to call a press conference. I just want to get it first."

Alex drew his hand over his eyes. He looked nerve-wracked and exhausted.

"I guess I can't stop you."

He bowed his head and raised his hand to his eyes again, before reaching for the doorknob. It couldn't be easy, having his sting operation end in homicide. Instead of being the hero who nailed Snake, he'd have to answer a lot of questions about what went wrong. I knew the media would be all over it. I would be, too. That was our job.

I wanted to call him back, but I didn't know what to say. I waited for the door to close behind him and stepped to the window. Gloom gathered in the woods outside. The rain continued to pour down. I called the newsroom.

"Dad?" I said. "I've got a scoop."

Twenty-four

Her Majesty's Coast Guard Ship *Joshua Slocum* was hardly the *Rainbow Warrior*. But later that evening it carried out a mission worthy of Greenpeace. It released Nyota back into the wild.

Canadian Wildlife Service Officer Margaret Chen, who was called in to take charge of Dr. Wallis' collection, let me take pictures while she and Ms. Cameron fitted the turtle with a GPS transmitter. The transmitter was built into a backpack contraption that made Nyota look like a poster-child for Mountain Equipment Co-op. Apparently it was more humane than drilling bolt-holes into her shell. So Ernest had been right about that, after all. Go figure.

It was cool and windy, but the rain had stopped. Ms. Cameron worked in silence. I knew she was upset that Dr. Wallis had turned out to be a criminal. I sensed she wasn't happy, either, that the news would be all over Nova Scotia by the time Dad posted the story on the Web. I felt bad for her, but my feelings didn't matter. My job was to report the story.

"What's going to happen to the other animals?" I asked the wildlife officer.

"We'll try to find some homes for them in zoos," she answered. "I wish we could release them all back into the wild, but we can't do that. Not after they've been in captivity for so long."

She paused and fiddled with the backpack's harness.

"The worst thing about these collectors is, they think they're not doing anything wrong," she continued. "But every time they take an endangered animal out of the wild, it drives that species a little closer to extinction. And the closer the species gets to extinction, the more these collectors will pay to get their hands on whatever animals are left. That's what drives the black market. And once a black-market ring is established, those criminals will smuggle drugs and weapons, too. These collectors, they don't realize the harm they're doing. And all on the backs of innocent animals. It makes me want to cry."

She finished tightening the backpack, tested the transmitter, and turned to Ms. Cameron.

"Ready?"

"Ready."

Nyota seemed eager to get back into the water, scrabbling with her awkward flippers over the deck. I met her yellow eyes, but I had no idea whether she recognized me, whether she knew that we were trying to help her.

"Good luck, sister," I whispered.

The camera on my phone wasn't exactly professional-caliber gear and I knew my pics would be pretty lousy, between the low evening light and the unsteady rocking of the boat, but I shot a couple dozen frames, just to put the moment on the record. It barely took a push from Ms. Cameron and Officer Chen to slip the turtle over the side, into the blackness of the ocean. She was gone; the only trace of her from now on would be a signal on a computer screen.

Ms. Cameron and Officer Chen gathered their equipment and climbed into the pilothouse for the trip back to shore.

I went to join Alex, who was leaning over the railing in the bow, staring up at the shifting gray clouds. I didn't stand too close to him, so he didn't have to talk if he didn't want to. But he spoke first.

"Did you file your story?"

"Yeah," I said.

"Am I in it?"

"Not by name."

"Thanks for that."

I shrugged. "Sergeant Arsenault's in charge of media relations. Right?"

Alex nodded.

"Right."

"So what happens now?" I asked.

"Off the record?"

"You won't tell me anything on the record, right?"

"Correct."

"Okay then. Off the record."

"We haven't charged Wallis. If we do, he'll plead self-defense. We'll have to consult with the Crown Prosecutor's office, but I don't think anyone wants to drag the old man through a trial."

"The jury'll never convict," I said. "He killed a drug dealer. They'll probably give him a medal."

"Yeah, but still—"

"A lot of dirt would come out." I thought of Dr. Wallis' 'collection.'

"Yeah," said Alex. "A lot."

"I'm not sure I understand why he shot Snake," I said. "If Doctor Wallis was behind this whole smuggling ring, why would he want to protect Ms. Cameron? Or Ernest? Why wouldn't he shoot them instead, and get rid of the witnesses?"

"I think the old professor got in over his head," Alex said. "From what he's been telling us, it seems like he started out importing exotic animals with a few contacts he had overseas. At first it was just for his private collection. Then some other collectors started asking if he could get them this or that, and the operation got bigger. More overseas contacts. More people bringing stuff in. It was like a passion for him. I don't think he ever saw it as a business. Let alone a criminal business."

"So he shot Snake to protect Ernest and Ms. Cameron?"

"Yeah. He was a decent man underneath."

"What about the drugs?"

"I think that was Snake's thing. He was probably already dealing, small-time. Then he got connected into Wallis' smuggling operation somehow. He got to know all the guys involved. He saw an opportunity and he exploited it. Started importing more and more stuff. Grew his network. I'm not sure that Dr. Wallis even knew about the drugs."

"I hope not."

"Yeah," said Alex.

"What about Tyler Dervish?"

"Good question. Wallis said he didn't know anything about it. If you want to know what I think, Snake killed him over the drug debt. Gil and Snake took the body out on the *Magdelaine* and dumped it somewhere at sea. It'll never be found now. And since Snake's dead and Gil's not talking, we'll never know for sure. But I'll bet the forensics guys will find some kind of evidence that puts Snake at the scene of the crime—blood or DNA or maybe a fingerprint. That's probably enough to close the case."

"Yeah," I said, thinking of Tyler, the skinny, runty kid with bad skin who wanted so badly to be cool. What a waste of life. He was young, maybe he could've still turned it around. Or maybe he would've grown up to be a guy like Snake.

I looked out over the ocean for a bit, feeling the wind and the sea spray. Watching the sky darken from twilight to night. Maybe I was getting to be a bit of a sucker for Mother Nature, because it felt nice being out there. Soothing.

"What about Captain Gil?" I said finally.

"He's been cooperative," said Alex. "We're going to try to help him out. Get him a fishing license for the West coast. The Queen Charlottes."

"Isn't it all Native land up there?"

"He's part Haida Indian, you know."

"He is not."

"He is now." Alex cracked about a quarter of a smile. I looked at him and smiled, too.

"I know you reporters like to ask all the questions," he said. "But I was wondering if I could ask you one."

My pulse throbbed in my neck. I looked out over the ocean.

"Sure."

"I was wondering if you wanted to go out with me sometime."

My heartbeat hammered in my eardrums. I couldn't look at him, even though I wanted to.

"We could grab a coffee..." I sounded like an idiot.

"I was thinking more like a dinner date."

Alex touched my hand.

"I'm not really into the dating scene —"

"I'm not a scene, Hayley. I'm just a guy."

I snuck a glimpse at him through the corner of my eye. Every part of him that I saw, I wanted to touch: the short, soft hairs at the nape of his neck, the stubble on the line of his jaw, the hair that fell in a fringe over his left eyebrow, the muscles that rippled in two long, smooth ridges down his back on either side of his spine. I wanted to trace those ridges from the curve of his shoulders down to his hips…

How could I feel so warm and so cold at the same time? My fingers trembled, my insides melted. My face burned. I turned my eyes away.

This is what gets girls into trouble.

You're scared.

No I'm not. I'm protecting myself.

Against what?

Against what happened to my mother.

You're not your mother.

No. I'm not. I'm not my mother.

I'm not a drunken sixteen-year-old runaway.

And Alex…he's not like any guy I've ever met.

He's not a goofy high school kid like Chuck and Phil. Not an immature nerd like Ernest. Not cocky like Trevor or creepy like Tyler Dervish.

Alex is nice. And smart. And…trustworthy. Yes, I think he's trustworthy.

I nestled my hand a little closer into his and it felt frightening and comforting both at once.

"I like you, Hayley," he said.

He caught my eyes with his, and they were soft and brown and gorgeous.

"Was that off the record?" I asked. Keeping it light. Making a little joke. Giving him a way out, if he wanted to take it.

"No way." He cupped my cheek with his hand. His lips touched mine with a warmth that made my heart roll over and surrender. "You can quote me on that."

Author's Note

When I started working on this book over a decade ago, I had no idea how to write a novel.

As I struggled to learn (the hard way) the rudiments of characterization, plotting, story arc, and voice, successive manuscripts were ripped up, scribbled over, shoved into the back of filing cabinets or stowed away for long periods of dormancy on floppy discs (remember those?). During that time, my life was moving forward and I was learning the ropes of daily journalism, first as a reporter at the *New Brunswick Telegraph-Journal* and later at the *Ottawa Citizen*. I'm at a very different place now than when I began this book: a mother of two children, working as an independent freelancer instead of a daily newshound. But I'm glad I never abandoned the manuscript, because Hayley reminds me of who I was as a cub reporter. I'm glad she'll have a life and a voice in this book.

There are so many people to thank and acknowledge along the way.

First, a shout-out to all my colleagues at the *Telegraph-Journal* and the *Ottawa Citizen*. I'm not sure if it's gone for good, but my time in the newsroom was the best of times.

Thanks to all of my colleagues in fiction writing, and especially to the members of my original writing group: Noreen, Mark, Rachel, Deb, Connie, and Michelle. At last, we witness the publication of "the novel formerly known as the dead boyfriend novel."

A big thank you to former Canadian Wildlife Service officer Wayne Turpin for reading an early draft of this manuscript and offering his professional insight. Any remaining errors or inaccuracies are my fault, not his.

Thanks, as always, to my supportive family and my wonderful husband Mark.

I'd also like to thank— without (much) irony—the editors and agents who rejected previous drafts of this manuscript. You were right. It needed more work. To those who took the time to give constructive feedback, my gratitude. Your insights helped me to strengthen the story.

And to Ellen Larson at Poisoned Pencil Press, thank you eternally for accepting my manuscript at a time when I had almost given up hope of publication. Thank you for your light and incisive touch in the editing process, for your enthusiasm in promoting the book, and for the personal connection that you've made and nurtured with me and the other Poisoned Pencil authors.

It's been a long road, but seeing the book in print makes it all worthwhile.

To receive a free catalog of Poisoned Pen Press titles, please provide your name and address through one of the following ways:

Phone: 1-800-421-3976
Facsimile: 1-480-949-1707
Email: info@poisonedpenpress.com
Website: www.poisonedpenpress.com

Poisoned Pen Press / The Poisoned Pencil
6962 E. First Ave. Ste 103
Scottsdale, AZ 85251

CPSIA information can be obtained at www.ICGtesting.com
Printed in the USA
LVOW11s1738240815

451315LV00006B/751/P